EARLY ONE MORNING

EARLY ONE MORNING

Pamela Oldfield

This first world edition published in Great Britain 2001 by
SEVERN HOUSE PUBLISHERS LTD of
9–15 High Street, Sutton, Surrey SM1 1DF.
This first world edition published in the USA 2001 by
SEVERN HOUSE PUBLISHERS INC of
595 Madison Avenue, New York, N.Y. 10022.

British Library Cataloguing in Publication Data

Oldfield, Pamela, 1934–
  Early one morning
  3. Horse racing – England – Epsom – Fiction
  2. Love stories
  I. Title
  823.9'14 [F]

ISBN 0-7278-5701-0

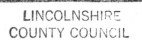

Typeset by Palimpsest Book Production Ltd.,
Polmont, Stirlingshire, Scotland.
Printed and bound in Great Britain by
MPG Books Ltd., Bodmin, Cornwall.

To Doreen and John,
with love

One

N ancy went down to breakfast with her fingers crossed. She was hoping that her stepmother had decided to have her meal in bed as she sometimes did. Sharing breakfast with Lilian was never conducive to good digestion and on this particular morning Nancy was feeling at peace with the world and hoped to stay that way. She had swept up her hair and wore a pale lilac blouse and darker skirt.

As soon as she opened the breakfast-room door she knew she was out of luck. Lilian turned from the sideboard and gave Nancy a cool smile.

'Good morning, Lilian.' Nancy returned the smile.

Lilian sat down with her eggs and bacon and reached for the toast. 'Is it today that the dressmaker's coming?'

'Yes. At ten o'clock.' This time Nancy's smile was genuine. Mrs Bailey was bringing Nancy's wedding dress for its first fitting.

'A pity. I'm expecting Laura Jennings but never mind.' She sighed. 'We'll have to find another room.'

That won't be too difficult, thought Nancy. Franklin Manor had six reception rooms as well as seven bedrooms. She helped herself to kidneys and tomatoes and took her place at the table. Lilian poured her a cup of tea and passed it across the table without comment. Her father's second wife was undeniably a beauty with blonde hair and deep blue

1

eyes below long, dark lashes – which she used to marvellous effect. She had earned Nancy's undying distrust by trying to charm Lawrence, her fiancé.

Nancy's looks were in another league altogether but her face was softened by gentle brown eyes and framed with dark curls.

For a few moments they ate in silence until Theo came into the room, his face flushed with excitement. Beneath his right arm he carried a small wooden horse. It was grey with white spots and the black mane was almost worn away. The tail had long since disappeared and Nanny had replaced it by gluing on some black wool. The horse, which went by the name of Thunder, was the boy's constant companion.

'You've left the door open,' Lilian told him.

He grinned as he turned to close it. 'Sorry, Mama.'

'Is your father coming in to breakfast?'

'He isn't hungry, Mama.'

Lilian rolled her eyes. 'What's the matter with the man? He hardly eats these days. It's not natural.'

Ignoring this grumble, Theo went on cheerfully. 'I was down in the stables watching the second string come back from the gallops.' He looked at Nancy. 'Gordie Brae went like the wind. Father thinks he might run him at Newmarket.'

Theodore was nine years old and the image of his mother. He had a dazzling smile and, to quote his father, could 'already charm the birds from the trees'. Nancy, the daughter of James Franklin's first wife, was thirteen years older than Theo but in spite of the gap they were very close. Nancy sometimes felt more like Theo's mother than his sister. It irked her that Lilian had never pretended to have maternal feelings and had made no secret that giving James a son had been a matter of duty. She seemed content to leave Theo's upbringing to others and was rarely to be seen when he was ill.

If James had any qualms about his young wife he kept them to himself. It seemed to Nancy that in his eyes the beautiful Lilian could do no wrong. At first Nancy had resented her efforts to replace her mother but since her own betrothal to Lawrence Wilton her stepmother's behaviour had troubled her less and less.

Theo continued as he lifted various lids on the sideboard in search of his preferred breakfast. 'It must be sad for poor old Tad, seeing all the other horses galloping while he has to stand and watch.'

Short in the leg and broad in the back, Tad was the hack favoured by James when he rode out to watch the gallops. He was the same age as Theo and had never been anything but a work horse.

'Don't be silly,' said Lilian. 'He has a very comfortable life. Plenty of food and nothing much to do.'

Theo carried his plate to the table. 'No sausages,' he grumbled.

'Children all over the world are starving,' Lilian told him. 'Be thankful for what you have, Theo.'

He rolled his eyes and risked a quick glance in Nancy's direction. She resisted the impulse to undermine her step-mother and said, 'Your mama's right, Theo.'

The boy placed his horse on the empty chair beside him.

'Cocksparrow's got heat in his shoulder,' he announced. 'Father's going to call the vet in.'

Lilian frowned. 'Cocksparrow? Is that the Demarrs' horse?'

Theo shook his head. 'He belongs to Colonel Harding. You know, Mama. The roan four-year-old. When the lad took off his blanket this morning there was a damp patch. Papa says it's heat in the muscle so he may not be able to run him.'

Nancy nodded but her thoughts had reverted to the wedding gown Mrs Bailey was making for her. She had chosen a heavy cream satin with a deeper lace for the bodice and hem. 'Too dark altogether,' Lilian had insisted but Nancy had thought ivory too cold for her warmer skin tones. Today the dressmaker would bring the tacked bodice and sleeves for a first fitting. The wedding was ten weeks away but nobody wanted a last-minute hitch and the dress was Nancy's main preoccupation.

Lilian was managing the rest of the arrangements. The guest list had been drawn up and the invitations designed to her satisfaction. Flowers would be ordered nearer the time and the caterers would be instructed. Cook would be busy with extra help brought in from the village. Nancy had to admit that her stepmother's organisational skills were enviable.

'So will your father be back for breakfast?' Lilian enquired.

Theo, his mouth full, could only nod.

'Good. I need to talk to him about Mrs Callender.'

Nancy caught something in the tone of voice and looked up. 'What about her?' she asked. 'Nanny's quite happy.'

'Her happiness is not in question, Nancy. But it is for me and your father to discuss.'

Theo swallowed and said, 'When I'm ten, can I have a gun for my birthday?'

Nancy and Lilian turned as one to stare at him.

Lilian said, 'A gun? I should think not! Whatever gave you that idea?'

Theo thrust out his lower lip. 'But Papa has a gun. It's not fair.'

Nancy said, 'Theo, boys don't have guns, only grown men. Papa needs one to scare away burglars or poachers. I thought you wanted a puppy.'

'Mama says I can't have a puppy because I'll be away at school and she'll have to look after it.'

4

'Well, what about a kitten? Cats look after themselves most of the time.'

Lilian tutted. 'You know I don't care for pets, Nancy. Do let him eat his breakfast.'

But Theo was in one of his awkward moods. 'But if Papa *says* I can have a gun . . .'

At that moment, as if on cue, James Franklin entered the room. He was out of breath, his greying hair was tousled and his cheeks were ruddy from the morning's exertion. He was a sturdy fellow and moved with the comfortable gait of the countryman. Nancy regarded him through narrowed eyes. In spite of the early morning exercise he looked tired, she thought. If only she had been born a boy. By now she would have been helping him manage the stables.

He poured himself a cup of tea and sat down at the head of the table.

Lilian wasted no time. 'We must talk about the boy's nanny, James. She really is—'

James said, 'I've told you before, dear, there is no need for changes. Nanny stays with us.'

Nancy busied herself with her food but she felt a rush of anxiety. What was Lilian talking about? Moira Callender had been with them for twenty-two years and had cared for both the Franklin children. Now she was in her eighties and losing her sight.

Theo put the last piece of his bacon into his mouth, chewed rapidly and swallowed. 'Mayberry threw Willem off this morning and he fell into some stinging nettles and the other lads laughed and Willem said a very rude word.' He grinned. 'I'm *not* going to say the word, Papa.'

'I should hope not!'

'But then Willem said that Mayberry is one of the worst horses he has ever ridden and God help his jockeys!'

Suddenly he had all their attention. James stiffened.

5

'Sorry, Papa!' Theo clamped a hand over his mouth but it was too late.

His father pointed to the door. 'Go up to your room and stay there until dinnertime!'

Theo glanced hopefully at his mother but she shrugged her slender shoulders.

James said, '*Now*, Theo.'

'He did apologise, Papa.'

Lilian glared at her. 'You always have to interfere, Nancy.'

Her father hesitated. 'Well, for half an hour then.'

Bowing to the inevitable, Theo slid from his chair and made his way to the door. Once there he threw Nancy an appealing look but she ignored it. She had done all she could for him and had no wish to irritate her father.

They all listened to the boy's footsteps as he stamped his way up the stairs. Nancy hid a smile but Lilian made disapproving sounds.

'You're much too soft with him,' she told her husband. 'And that school's doing him no good at all. His manners get worse and worse. And about his nanny—'

Nancy said, 'What about her? She's quite happy here.'

'Miss Callender should be with her family.'

Nancy stared at her in dismay. 'But she has no family. You know that. She was an only child and never married.'

'That is hardly our concern. She was employed here as a nanny but she has outgrown her usefulness.'

'That's not the point,' Nancy exploded. 'We owe her such a lot. She cared for me when Mama died and she helped you with Theo. Surely we have a debt of duty—'

'She needs a full-time nurse.'

'Oh no!' Nancy looked at her father in alarm. 'You know she would hate that. She values her independence. It would make her feel like an invalid.'

'She *is* an invalid.' Lilian's mouth was set in a stubborn line.

James said, 'Nancy's right, darling. She's very proud and I should hate to—'

Lilian gave him a strange look. 'You never consider me, do you, James. Never.'

Nancy and James stared at her. This was a new complaint.

She went on, 'You never wonder whether or not it is fair for me to bear yet another burden. As long as your life is uninterrupted. You live for the stables and your damned horses, James, and I come a very poor second.' She was breathing rapidly, her chest heaving. 'I might just as well be your housekeeper.'

Nancy dared not look at her father. The conversation was becoming very personal and she felt she shouldn't be part of it. But how was she to extricate herself?

'I am entitled to a life of my own, you know,' Lilian went on, her blue eyes dark with resentment.

Nancy said, 'But Cook and I do most of the running up and down. She usually takes Nanny's meal trays up and sometimes I do it, and when Theo's home from school he loves to bring down the tray. You don't understand, Lilian. Theo adores Nanny. He reads to her in his fashion and—'

Lilian's expression hardened. 'Please don't take that tone with me, Nancy. You have no idea how much I do or how little I am appreciated. For the last few months you have been so wrapped up in your wedding that everything has fallen on my shoulders. And since you will be gone from here in a few months it really doesn't concern you.'

Nancy looked at her father. 'But it does. Papa . . . ?'

James turned to his wife. 'I've said no, Lilian, to the idea of her leaving us. There is nothing more to talk about.'

Lilian's cheeks flared with angry colour. 'Oh, I see. It's another little conspiracy, isn't it, between you and your precious daughter! And your foolish old woman. I'm your wife but I've ceased to matter, haven't I? You promised so much when we were wed but now . . .' She drew in a sharp breath. 'Everyone's so worried about Mrs Callender and her happiness but no one bothers about me. If I'm not happy, James – and I'm not – you have only yourself to blame.'

Nancy listened with growing astonishment. Surely Lilian led a cosseted life with her bridge parties, afternoon teas on the terrace with her cronies and endless trips to London to scour the shops in Oxford Street.

James's face had reddened. He said, 'As far as I'm concerned, Nanny is part of the family. I'll consider a nurse for her. I don't want her to be a burden to you, Lilian.'

Lilian threw down her napkin and stood up. 'Moira Callender is not one of *my* family, but you're welcome to her.'

James was holding down his anger with difficulty. 'I hope you haven't spoken to her about this?'

Lilian hesitated and Nancy guessed at once that she had. 'I shall go up and see Nanny right now,' she said. 'And set her mind at rest.'

Her father avoided her eyes but Lilian made no attempt to hide her annoyance. As Nancy left the room she heard Lilian say, 'That girl of yours is much too forward, James. I'm afraid you've spoiled her.'

Pausing outside the door, Nancy listened for her father's reply but the words were not clear enough. As she went up the stairs she fought back her anger. She was going to be fitted for her wedding dress and she must not allow Lilian to spoil her day. As she thought of Lawrence her spirits lifted and a smile lit her face. Mrs Lawrence Wilton. The next ten weeks couldn't go fast enough.

Franklins, a racing stable on the outskirts of Epsom, was well respected and their twenty stalls were never empty.

Horses were brought to James Franklin from far and wide, their owners assured of the best possible treatment for their precious thoroughbreds. James Franklin had inherited the stables from his father and had planned to share it with his son since the day Theo was born. The fact that his first child was a daughter had been a huge disappointment but he'd come to terms with his lot and adored Nancy. When his first wife, Alice, died he had remained a widower for five years, concentrating all his efforts on the stables. He had not intended to remarry until he met Lilian, who immediately fascinated him. To the astonishment of the racing fraternity, he had pursued her relentlessly until she agreed to become his wife. Theo had satisfied his longing for an heir but Lilian had made it clear there would be no more children.

Financially Franklins, as it was known, was a hundred per cent sound and its reputation meant that they could employ excellent staff. They had seven stable lads, one stable jockey by the name of Deakes, and Jack Liddy as head lad. This last title was misleading for the position of head lad carried enormous responsibilities for the day-to-day running of the stables, the supervision of the lads and, most importantly, the well-being of the horses. He was, in fact, the most important person after the owner and James considered Jack Liddy vital to the success of the business.

As James made his way back towards the stables he pushed the problem of Moira Callender to the back of his mind. He was trying to forget his wife's accusations but her hostility had shocked him. Had he neglected her? he wondered. Wasn't it enough that he worked all the hours God gave and that he made very comfortable provision for his family? True, he had married a young social butterfly but he had expected motherhood to provide a satisfying alternative role for her.

'Oh, Lilian!' he muttered. If only there were more hours in the day. He still loved her dearly but there were so many demands on his time. Sighing, he entered the stableyard and the businessman took over from the husband. David Evans, the vet, was due at any moment and there was work to be done.

Theo rushed to meet him. 'Mr Liddy says Bay Lover is pining and he thinks we should get him a companion. Can we, Papa?'

One of the lads, passing with a bridle over one arm, laughed at the boy's enthusiasm. 'Why don't you volunteer, then, Master Theodore? Bay Lover likes you. You could share his stable.'

'Oh no, Fred!' Taking this suggestion seriously, Theo tried to explain. 'Mr Liddy meant an animal. A donkey, perhaps.'

James ruffled his son's hair. 'Fred's teasing you, Theo.'

The lad went on his way, grinning, and Theo looked relieved. 'But could we buy a donkey for him? He's so sad.'

'Sad, is he?'

'He's not eating properly and Mr Liddy says he's bad-tempered.'

They stopped in the middle of the cobbled yard and James surveyed the scene with a critical eye. The large yard was surrounded on three sides by stalls for the horses and each row had its own tack room. Six horses were being groomed by their lads and were shuffling their hooves, rolling their eyes and tossing their heads as they wound down after the excitement of the morning's gallop. The lads were busy with buckets of warm water, cloths, curry-combs and brushes and each horse's lathered coat was being restored to a satisfactory gleam. No lad would skimp on the work. It was a matter of pride that when James Franklin did his rounds the horses would look their best.

Beyond the stables on the left was a large barn which housed the feedstuff, hay and other materials. The governess cart and the four-wheeled wagonette were also kept there. As James strode in this direction Theo ran alongside, chattering excitedly about the proposed donkey.

James stopped. 'I don't care for donkeys, Theo, but what do you think of a goat, eh? They are much more tractable. You could think of a name for it and when you're at home you can look after it.'

Theo gazed up at him and James had to resist the unmanly urge to throw his arms round him. He was so like his mother and yet there were times when a fleeting expression or a turn of the head would remind James of himself as a boy. On the surface Theo was a cheerful boy but there was a vulnerability hidden within him which James recognised with regret.

Theo hesitated. 'A goat? A goat would be nice . . . A donkey would be better but—' Seeing his father's expression he came to a quick decision. 'A goat, Papa. Bay Lover would love that.'

'Then a goat it is. Run and tell Mr Liddy while I have a word with Symes, and then I must take a look at Cocksparrow.'

The boy hurried away, full of importance – the bearer of exciting news. James entered the barn. George Symes, the gardener-cum-handyman, was polishing the wagonette and took the chance to stop and wipe his face with the red handkerchief that had become his trademark. Nancy always said she was sure that he took the handkerchief to bed with him and would want it to share his coffin when the time came. He was a large man in his early fifties, a little overweight but very strong in the arms.

'Mornin', Mr Franklin, sir.'

'Good morning, Symes.'

Symes frowned suddenly and bent forward, clutching his stomach.

'What's up, man?' James was immediately concerned.

'Bit of a twinge.' He straightened up cautiously. 'Belly-ache. It's nothing.'

'You get yourself seen to.'

'Probably a bit of indigestion, sir.'

'You get the doctor to check you out.'

'Will do, sir.' He took a few deep breaths and then nodded towards the wagonette. It was a new model, brown with black and yellow wheels. 'Just giving it a bit of a polish. The mistress wants it this afternoon. Off on one of her . . . her little jaunts, I dare say.'

'Oh? Did she say where she was going?'

'Oh no, sir. Not for me to ask.' He stared at his yellow duster. 'The mistress don't tell me nothing.'

Losing interest, James looked up at the cross-beams. His first wife had been a talented amateur artist and had chosen the interior of the barn as the subject of four of her pictures. Today she would have painted a fifth, he thought. The bright June sunlight slanted through gaps in the wooden walls, fell across bales of golden straw and warmed the red tones of the brick floor. He had first kissed Alice in this barn and could still remember the sweet smell of her hair as he took her into his arms. Lilian was a beauty but Alice had been his first sweetheart and he would always miss her.

He became aware that Symes was talking to him about a split in the wagonette's leather seat and forced the memories to the back of his mind. They talked over one or two problems but five minutes later James heard the approach of the vet's pony trap and hurried back to the stables. David Evans was a thick-set man, short in the leg. His face was like old leather but his faded blue eyes missed very little. No one knew his age but he was no longer young and was going a little deaf.

An equally ancient spaniel accompanied him in the trap and the sound of his frenzied barking brought Theo at a run. It was the boy's job to take the old dog for a walk so that the horses were not disturbed by his presence. Theo, full of importance, clipped the lead to the dog's collar and led him briskly away.

Together James and Evans examined Cocksparrow.

'He's favouring the off fore leg,' James explained.

'Mmm . . . Could be a hairline fracture.'

'Let's hope not. The damp patch was on the same shoulder. I'm thinking there might be heat in the muscle.'

'First time you've noticed it?'

'His lad said he might have been moving awkwardly yesterday but he wasn't sure. We ran him about a week ago and he was fine. Came in a good second.'

'Came in what?'

'I said he came in a good second.'

'Ah! Hmm . . .' He straightened up. 'Well, it may not be much. Give him a week's rest. No gallops, mind. Just a walk round the yard from time to time. If it's no better I'll look in again.' He patted the horse's slender neck. 'Colonel Harding's horse, isn't it?'

'One of them. We have two of his. Gold Fever is the other one.'

'The big roan?'

James nodded.

For the next half-hour they went from stall to stall, chatting about the various horses until David Evans pulled out his watch.

'I must go.' He glanced round. 'Now where's that dog of mine?'

'He'll be waiting at the far gate, I expect.'

'Waiting where?'

'At the far gate – with Theo. I'll walk with you.'

Minutes later James watched until the trap was out of sight and turned back to his stable. Jack Liddy, an ancient trilby hat set at a rakish angle on his thinning hair, appeared from one of the tack rooms and asked about the verdict.

13

'Let's hope the colonel doesn't decide to telephone,' he said when James had passed on the vet's comments.

James agreed. Of all the Franklin owners Colonel Harding was the fussiest. Six days out of seven he would find any excuse to telephone the stable but since he was considering buying a third horse for them to train, James was willing to humour him. Now, with Theo chattering beside him, James set off in the direction of the house. The horses were in good hands and there was always paperwork piling up in the office, awaiting his attention.

At quarter past ten, wearing the top half of her wedding dress, Nancy made her way up the stairs and along the corridor to Nanny's room. She tapped on the door and entered. If Nanny was dozing, she would wake her up.

'Nancy dear!' The old lady struggled upright in her chair and clutched at one of the cushions, which was about to fall. She held a piece of embroidery in her other hand but Nancy knew that very few stitches were added these days. Perhaps it was an attempt to pretend she was still capable – intended to impress Lilian, possibly. Moira Callender was small and had once been round but no longer. She's fading away, thought Nancy with a sense of shock.

Nancy crossed the room to help her replace the cushion.

'I mustn't be long,' she said. 'Mrs Bailey is downstairs waiting for your approval! What do you think?' She turned slowly on her heel to show off the bodice.

'Oh my dear!' Nanny clasped her hands, her eyes shining with delight. 'It's a perfect fit. It's going to be beautiful! Tell Mrs Bailey I'm full of admiration. Tell her that her needle is as nimble as her tongue!' She looked hopefully at Nancy. 'Anything interesting today?'

Mrs Bailey was the village gossip. Nothing escaped her eagle eye.

'Not much,' Nancy told her. 'Unless you remember

the butcher's daughter. The older one. She's expecting a baby.'

The old lady shook her head as Nancy continued to show off the bodice. It fitted high on the neck and the sleeves reached to her wrists. 'This is just the under-layer,' Nancy explained. 'The lace goes over the top.'

'You're going to look like a princess! Oh, I do wish I could be there to see you married!'

'But of course you'll be there. You can't miss my big day.'

Nanny looked flustered. 'Oh dear! I mean, will I really? I know it will be difficult . . .'

Nancy felt a familiar rush of indignation. This sounded like more of Lilian's doing. 'Of course it won't be difficult,' she said. 'How could it be? We'll carry you down the stairs and into the carriage. We're hiring a brougham. I couldn't get married without you! It's unthinkable.' She patted the thin arm.

Nanny's face had cleared. 'I'm so glad. I'm counting the days, you know,' she said. 'I just hope Master Lawrence knows how lucky he is!' She clasped her hands in front of her chest and beamed up at Nancy.

'He does, I'm sure,' Nancy told her. 'I shall see him this afternoon. I've challenged him to a round of croquet and he's coming to lunch beforehand. Shall I give him your best wishes?'

'Please do, dear. I always have liked him. Ever since he was a boy and the two of you used to play together.' Her voice grew wistful. 'Such nice manners, I remember, and so considerate. A real little gentleman. Not that Theo isn't, you understand – he's a dear little man – but he's a different generation and things change.' She sighed. 'Do you remember that picnic by the pool? It was your tenth birthday and Master Lawrence was invited. No one else. You only wanted him; you insisted.' She smiled. 'It was

15

very windy but you insisted on going ahead with the picnic. Your straw hat blew into the water and Master Lawrence waded straight in after it.'

'And handed it back to me, sopping wet, expecting me to wear it again!' Nancy laughed.

Nanny nodded. 'I thought then that his heart must be in the right place . . . but I must stop calling him Master Lawrence. I keep forgetting. He's grown up now and will soon be a married man. I must call him Mr Wilton.'

Nancy sat on the bed beside her old nanny, delighted by the opportunity to talk about Lawrence. Her father was too busy to talk about her feelings for the man she was going to marry and Lilian showed little interest in the subject. Nancy half suspected that her stepmother was a little jealous. Lawrence Wilton was every girl's dream. Tall, good-looking and very charming, he wore his wavy brown hair parted in the middle and his voice was rarely raised in anger. When Nancy looked into his hazel eyes she could deny him nothing – not that he asked more than a chaste kiss and an arm around her waist. He was a member of the highly respected Wilton family that had lived nearby on Mannington Farm for more than two hundred years. They owned nearly a thousand acres and hunted regularly. There was nobody for miles around who did not respect the family – with the exception of one or two poachers who stole game from the woods or took trout from the river.

Nanny said, 'I'm so pleased you're happy, dear. I'm sure your Mr Wilton will give you everything you deserve in life.' Her eyes gleamed. 'Including a brood of handsome children!'

'Nanny!'

They exchanged knowing smiles although 'knowing' was hardly the right word. Nanny had never been married and presumably knew nothing about the duties of the marriage bed. Nancy also remained in almost total ignorance. The thought of asking Lilian for help was anathema to her and her stepmother had never suggested a 'little talk'. Nancy had worried over the subject but had come to the conclusion that whatever Lawrence asked of her she would give willingly. He would know. She would trust him.

'Nanny,' she began carefully. 'Has my stepmother said anything to you about you . . . not staying on at Franklins?' The old lady's expression changed but before she could answer Nancy hurried on. 'Because if she has I don't want you to give it another thought. Papa and I are determined that you will stay with us and nothing my stepmother says will shake us.'

Nanny's mouth trembled slightly. 'But I do hate to be a burden. Mrs Franklin was right when she said that. I wish I had somewhere else to go but your mother did promise me—'

Nancy took hold of her hand. 'We wouldn't let you go even if you wanted to.' She smiled. 'You're part of our family now. Theo and I are very fond of you.'

Nanny still looked unconvinced. 'I'd never thought of myself as bedridden. I can walk a little and I get up every morning and sit in my chair. I dress myself . . . and I keep busy.' She held up her needlework by way of proof.

Nancy felt a rush of anger towards Lilian. 'It would make no difference if you were bedridden but you're nothing of the kind. The very idea! You are splendid for your age. Doctor Mayne always says how plucky you are.'

This wasn't strictly true but Nancy was trying to undo the harm done by Lilian's unkind words.

Nanny brightened. 'Plucky? Does he? Isn't that kind of him.'

'So no more worrying. Be reassured – you are staying with us.' She glanced at the bedside clock and jumped to her feet. 'I must fly. Poor Mrs Bailey will wonder what's keeping me. I'll tell her you approve the bodice, shall I?'

With a quick smile she hurried out, closing the door softly behind her. She longed to throttle her stepmother but instead decided she would talk to her father. He needed to be told that his pretty little wife could be very mean indeed.

Two

Lunchtime arrived and they were four. The table had been laid on the terrace and Lilian, Theo, Nancy and Lawrence sat down to eat. James had intended to join them but one of his owners had turned up unexpectedly, wishing to discuss the purchase of a new horse.

'It's John Brayde,' Lilian informed them. 'He already has four horses with us and two with another trainer but some people are never content.'

'It's a passion with some people,' said Lawrence. 'And Brayde's having a good season. Probably spending some of the money he won at Doncaster last week.'

Lilian glanced up suddenly. 'Was that the telephone?'

'I didn't hear anything,' Nancy told her.

Her stepmother seemed somewhat distracted, she thought curiously.

'Are you expecting a call?' she asked.

'No . . . that is, yes. But it's not important.'

At that moment Cook brought in a mixed salad, a large assortment of cold meats and a bowl of home-made pickles. There was a jug of iced water on the table and fresh rolls and butter.

Lilian frowned. 'Where's the champagne, Cook?'

Cook looked flustered. 'I didn't know – that is, I thought you were referring to tonight's meal.'

'That will be too late.'

'I'm sorry, ma'am. I'll go and fetch it.'

'And bring some suitable glasses.'

Nancy looked at Lilian. 'Are we celebrating?'

She opened her mouth to reply but Lawrence said quickly, 'We don't need an excuse to drink champagne. It's a very popular summer drink.'

Theo said, 'May I have a sip, Mama? I've never tasted champagne.'

'Don't be silly, Theo. You will drink water as usual.'

'So there is no special occasion?' Nancy persisted.

Lilian avoided her eyes. 'Lawrence has just explained that we don't need an occasion.' She helped herself to a minute portion of salad and a small slice of ham. 'I really can't face food,' she announced unnecessarily.

Nancy felt as though she had missed something intangible. Then it occurred to her that her stepmother might be expecting a second child. But for Lilian that would hardly be a cause for celebration. Giving birth to Theo had been, in her own words, a 'horrific nightmare' which she prayed would never be repeated. Nancy glanced at her stepmother. Did she imagine a brighter colour than usual in her cheeks? Had she heard agitation in her voice? She told herself she was imagining things and helped herself to salad and cold pork.

Lilian looked at her son who had slumped in his chair. 'And stop sulking, Theo. You really are a most trying creature.' She smiled apologetically at Lawrence. 'My husband has spoiled both his children,' she told him.

Lawrence said, 'Oh, surely not!' but Nancy let it pass.

Eager for the touch of her fiancé's hand, she wished they were sitting next to each other instead of either side of Theo. Still, he was here with her and that was wonderful.

Theo put a radish into his mouth and chewed it with obvious relish.

'I love radishes,' he told Lawrence. 'Matron says they're

good for us. The stronger the better! I could eat the strongest radish in the whole world.'

'Don't talk with your mouth full, Theo. I've told you a thousand times.'

Fortunately Theo ignored this exaggeration and Nancy breathed a sigh of relief. She wanted lunch to be pleasant and it wouldn't be if Theo and Lilian locked horns.

Theo turned to Lawrence. 'Papa is going to buy a goat and I'm going to call it Button. Do you see why?'

'Because he can butt people?' Lawrence suggested.

Theo smiled broadly. 'Yes. Isn't it a good name for a goat?'

'Shouldn't it be Butter?' Nancy suggested. 'Because—'

'Oh no! Because butter melts and goats don't.'

'Ah yes! I see that.'

Lilian said, 'I do hope Cook isn't on the telephone. She goes on and on. I heard her the other day speaking to the fishmonger. She was practically telling him her life story!'

As though to prove her wrong, Cook arrived with three glasses and a bottle of champagne.

Lilian asked Lawrence to do the honours and the 'pop' sent Theo dashing from his chair in search of the cork.

Lilian frowned. 'That school is too lenient,' she told Lawrence. 'Not enough discipline. I don't recommend it for your children when they arrive.'

Nancy cried, 'Lilian!'

Undeterred, her stepmother poured the champagne. 'I warned James. I suggested Fairways in Chester but he wouldn't even consider it.'

'But Hartleigh is Papa's old school,' Nancy protested. 'I would have gone there if I'd been a boy.'

Lawrence said, 'I think it's just high spirits, Mrs Franklin. Theo is a credit to you both.'

Nancy felt a rush of gratitude. Lawrence was so long-suffering. He couldn't enjoy this family bickering but he never allowed himself to show it. She made a mental note to ensure that when they did have a family she would not allow any quarrelling.

Theo returned to the table, the cork held aloft in triumph.

'It's good luck,' he told them, as he resumed his seat and placed it carefully on the table beside his plate. Then he picked it up and offered it to his mother. 'For you, Mama.'

For a long moment Lilian looked at him, her expression unfathomable. Slowly she reached out and accepted the cork. 'Thank you, Theo.' She looked as though she was about to say more but at that moment the church clock struck the half-hour and Lilian pushed back her chair. 'I have to make a telephone call,' she explained. 'Please do excuse me for a few moments.'

Puzzled, Nancy watched her hurry across the terrace and in through the French windows. As soon as her stepmother had disappeared, she reached across the table and Lawrence covered her hand with his. He mouthed the words 'I love you' and she did the same.

Theo said, 'You're whispering!' and helped himself to another slice of ham.

Lawrence said, 'I'm going to Dorset tomorrow for a couple of days to help a friend of mine. He's bought . . . that is, he needs some advice on a new property. I'd really rather not go but it's difficult to refuse a friend. I'll telephone you, of course.'

Nancy was overwhelmed with disappointment. Knowing that Lawrence lived so near made it bearable when they were apart. But Dorset was miles away and she was at once desperately jealous of his 'friend'. 'Is it anyone I know?'

'I doubt it.'

'Do goats like ham, Nancy?' Theo interrupted.

'I think they like everything.'

22

Lawrence said, 'We're going to play croquet this afternoon, Theo. You can play if you like – if Nancy doesn't mind.'

'I don't mind at all. I love beating Theo!'

'Why don't we play cricket?' Theo suggested. 'I'm very good at cricket. Much better than Marriot Minor. He can't catch for toffee but I can. And I can bat. Why can't we play cricket?'

'Because it's June,' Nancy told him, 'and I'm not going to race about in the hot sun. Croquet I can face.'

Theo put a last mouthful of salad into his mouth and laid his knife and fork side by side on the plate. 'Tommy likes us to put our knife and fork like this. If we remember we get house points. I'm not as good as Dunster but he's taller than me and so he's a better catcher. But I don't like him. His mother says horse racing's bad because it makes people gamble and then they haven't got any money left for their children's food and they have to go barefoot and it's criminal.'

Nancy opened her mouth to say something scathing about Mrs Dunster then changed her mind. It was obvious that comments made at home had an unpleasant way of reaching the wrong ears. Schools were notorious for the spreading of family gossip.

Cook arrived with a bowl of strawberries and a jug of cream. She was followed by Lilian who hovered nearby looking slightly agitated. Nancy gave Theo some strawberries and he helped himself to cream. Lawrence had seized the fly swatter and was busily driving away an early wasp.

'I'm afraid I have to go out,' Lilian told them. 'A small crisis which needs my attention. These charities take up more and more of my time.' For some reason she glanced quickly at Lawrence. 'Still, one does one's best for those less fortunate.'

Lawrence stammered, 'Indeed!'

'Now, if you will all excuse me.' As she turned to leave she caught sight of Theo's plate and rolled her eyes. 'Good Lord! How can you be so greedy, Theo? What an impossible child you are.' Suddenly she leaned down and kissed him. 'Goodbye, darling. Be good.'

Nancy watched Lilian walk briskly away. She looked at Lawrence but he was pouring the last of the champagne into her glass and didn't look up.

By seven thirty-five that same evening Nancy had supervised Theo's bath and had watched him clean his teeth. Now in his pyjamas, he was sitting upstairs with Nanny in her room while she read to him for fifteen minutes – a treat they both enjoyed during the holidays. Tomorrow the half-term break would be over and Lilian would take him back to school. Nancy was sitting in the drawing room, embroidering a white rose pattern on one of the pillowslips she was making as part of her trousseau. From time to time she glanced at the clock on the mantelpiece, her anxiety growing.

There was a knock on the door and Cook came into the room.

'I was wondering about dinner, Miss Nancy – the mistress not being home and everything.'

Nancy's anxiety deepened. 'Have you spoken to Papa?'

'Not yet. He's still doing his evening rounds at the stables. Leastways I guess so. I haven't seen hair nor hide of him since breakfast.'

Nancy hesitated. She was beginning to think there had been an accident. Lilian was never this late without a telephone call to reassure them of her whereabouts.

Cook went on, 'Only I'm ready to pop the lamb in and I don't want to ruin it.'

Nancy laid down her sewing. 'I'll find Papa and ask him,'

she said. 'Then I'll let you know. A few minutes here or there won't matter since we have no guests.'

She threw a shawl round her shoulders and set off for the stables. On the way she passed the barn and saw Symes closing the doors.

'Oh, you're back!' she cried. 'I was beginning to worry.' Turning, she retraced her steps and went into the kitchen. 'They're back,' she told Cook. 'You can go ahead with the meal.'

Cook looked surprised. 'Well now, I didn't see her come in. I must be going deaf as well as daft!'

It was one of her favourite expressions but Nancy smiled dutifully. As she left the kitchen she heard the meat tin slide into the oven and realised that she was hungry. The game of croquet had proved hilarious and had lasted longer than intended. All that fresh air, she told herself. She went into the drawing room to retrieve her pillowslip and pack it away in her sewing basket then made her way upstairs to say goodnight to Theo.

'When's Mama coming home?' he asked sleepily.

'Soon,' Nancy told him. 'She's a bit late so you can start your prayers without her if you wish.' She bent to kiss him.

'I want a goat that's white and brown,' he told her. 'Not all brown. All brown goats aren't so nice.'

'White and brown it shall be then. Remember to tell Papa tomorrow before you go back to school.'

'But if I don't see him . . . He's taking Mayberry to Newmarket for the two thirty and that's an early start.'

'Then I'll give him your message.'

As she went downstairs she met her father coming up. He was carrying a sheaf of papers and wore his usual frown. They didn't speak and Nancy went into her own room to change her dress.

Twenty minutes later, in the dining room, Nancy and

James waited for Lilian to appear. James looked ill at ease
and they sat in silence but when Cook brought in the soup he
snapped, 'Go up and find her, Nancy. Does she think we're
all going to sit here all night?'

Upstairs a shock awaited Nancy. There was no sign of her
stepmother. She went into Theo's room but he had fallen
asleep. Downstairs she broke the news to her father and they
stared at each other in incomprehension.

'But she must be here somewhere.' James stood up. 'What
on earth is she playing at?'

The soup cooled as the minutes passed and then alarm
bells began to ring.

Nancy said, 'They can't have had an accident because
Symes is back. I saw him outside the barn.'

'Damnation! I suppose we'll have to ask him.'

'I'll go. I might catch him in the kitchen if I'm lucky.'
Nancy could see how awkward it would be for her father
to have to ask the groom about Lilian.

In the kitchen Cook shook her head. 'Mr Symes hasn't
been in,' she told Nancy. 'I thought it a bit odd because
he always pops his head in the door before he goes home
in the hope there'll be a few leftovers. His wife's a dab
hand with them. Can make something really tasty out of
a bit of ham and some odds and ends—' She stopped as
she realised that something was wrong. 'What is it? Has
something happened?'

Nancy hesitated. 'It sounds ridiculous,' she said slowly,
'but . . . we can't find Mrs Franklin. She's not in the house.'
Distractedly she ran her fingers through her hair. 'I'll go
across to the cottage.'

With a shawl flung over her shoulders she set off across
the kitchen garden, past the orchard and the stables, arriving
at last at the small cottage where Symes and his wife and
children lived. A sharp knock brought Annie Symes to the
door. She was very pale and obviously agitated.

26

'Oh, Miss Nancy!' she cried, her voice louder than was necessary. Something in her eyes turned Nancy's unease into the beginnings of fear.

'I'd like to speak with your husband if he's here.'

'He's . . . That is, I don't think . . .' She clutched her apron nervously.

'It's rather important,' Nancy insisted with growing alarm.

'The fact is, miss, that he . . . I mean, you mustn't blame him. It was orders, Miss Nancy. *Her* orders, I mean. What was he to do? He didn't know how to . . . How could he say no?'

Nancy's heart skipped a beat. She had heard enough to realise that there was bad news on the way.

'If Mr Symes won't speak to me he will have to face my father. Now fetch him, please.' Her tone was deliberately sharp. Something was terribly wrong and the sooner they knew what it was the sooner they could deal with it.

Mrs Symes withdrew and a moment or two later her husband appeared. 'You'd best come in,' he muttered and led the way to a small parlour. It smelled damp, there was soot in the hearth and the brass fender hadn't been polished for months. Nancy remained standing and waited fearfully, bracing herself for whatever was to come.

He looks guilty, she thought as Symes rubbed his eyes.

'It wasn't up to me to gainsay the mistress,' he began. 'I just done what I was bid, that's all. 'Twas her that done wrong, Miss Nancy, begging your pardon, not me so there's no use blaming me.' His attempt at bravado was pathetic, undermined by the tremor in his voice. 'Mrs Franklin said "Go here", "Go there", and that's what I done. I'm the groom. The driver. I do what I'm told. Not up to me, Miss Nancy. Not my place to go tale-telling and I never did though I wanted to.'

His attitude was becoming aggrieved but Nancy detected something more behind the bluster.

'Out with it,' she told him. 'My father wants to know where his wife is and we think you must know.'

He refused to meet her gaze and stared at his feet instead, his mouth working silently. 'I dropped her off at the railway station and that's all I'm to say.'

'The railway station? I thought she was going to a meeting locally. That's what—' She stopped herself in time. 'And weren't you supposed to meet her when she returned?'

'No, miss. She said as how . . . She told me she wasn't coming back.' He looked up.

Nancy blinked. 'Not coming back? What on earth do you mean?'

He shrugged. 'That's what she said. But that's up to her. Nothing to do with me. 'Tis up to her, being the mistress.'

There was a deep coldness somewhere inside Nancy and she realised she was shivering. 'But . . . But she left here at lunchtime. When did you get back?'

There was a long silence. Then he said, 'Just after six, like I was told. "Go home around six", that's what she told me and that's what I done. Two shillings. That's what she gave me. I can't afford to turn down that kind of money. I've got a family to feed.' His expression had changed. The earlier bravado was giving way to fear, thought Nancy with a rush of pity.

They stared at each other while Nancy's brain buzzed with questions. At last she said, 'Has my stepmother ever given you money before?'

'Every Wednesday.' He swallowed. 'I don't deny it – but why shouldn't I take it? A tip's a tip. My wife said I should come tell you but I daren't and that's the truth. Every Wednesday she met him at the—'

'Him?'

'Yes. She met him at the station and I was to keep quiet and—'

'Met who at the station?' Nancy felt breathless with shock.

'Mr Cooper. Donald Cooper. Always there, he was, waiting with his buggy. She would run up to him and he'd put his arms around her and—'

'Stop!' cried Nancy, unable to hear any more. Feeling faint, she gulped for air and clutched the back of a chair for support.

'Are you all right, Miss Nancy?'

She nodded. She was afraid to hear more because she couldn't bear the thought of repeating it all to her father. How could she tell him Lilian had gone away with another man? Better for him to hear it from Symes himself, she told herself.

She straightened up cautiously, struggling to appear calm, testing the strength of her legs before she decided to walk anywhere. 'You'd better come up to the house – but not yet. Give me ten minutes to – to prepare my father.'

At that moment Annie Symes rushed into the room. Flushed with anxiety, she held one hand to her heart while the other clutched her apron. Her lips trembled.

'Please don't let your pa sack him, Miss Nancy!' she began but her husband caught her arm and tried to push her from the room.

'Leave this to me, Annie,' he told her but she forced her way back in.

'Please, Miss Nancy! I know he's done wrong but it's not fair to blame him and she's getting off scot-free! My husband's not to blame and maybe he shouldn't have kept the money but we needed it with another little 'un on the way. If your pa sacks him and we're thrown out of here—' Without warning she burst into tears, hiding her grief in her hands.

Nancy crossed the room and laid a hand on her trembling shoulder. She felt far from calm herself. 'I don't know what will happen but I'll do what I can. I can't begin to imagine what Papa will say or do.'

Unable to bear the intensity of Annie's sobs, Nancy pushed past her and her husband without ceremony, made her way out into the passage and let herself out. 'Ten minutes!' she called back and then hurried towards the house, the unwilling bearer of devastating news. Locked within herself she carried a sense of impending disaster.

In the orchard she paused for a moment or two to sort out her chaotic feelings and to decide how best to break the news. Had Lilian eloped? It certainly looked like it although it was hard to believe she would abandon Theo. If she had run off, would Papa go after her and bring her back? If she would come back. Suppose she refused to return . . .

'Oh, Lilian!' she muttered. 'How could you be such a fool?'

Slowly the pieces were falling into place. Now she understood the reason for Lilian's agitation and her eagerness for the telephone call. She had been waiting for some kind of prearranged signal from Donald Cooper. But it hadn't come so she had made the call herself.

'You fool!' she repeated.

Despairingly she looked around her, hardly seeing the elderly plum trees and the recently planted pear. It was frightening to stand in such a familiar place and know that nothing would ever be the same again. Even if Lilian could be brought home, she would never live down the disgrace of an elopement let alone that of leaving her child. And who would look after Theo? She, Nancy, would be gone in a few months from now and Nanny was too old and frail to care for another Franklin child. The questions crowded into her mind and Nancy groaned.

'Why? Why *now*?' she demanded aloud.

Selfishly she thought of the impact it would have on her own life. What should have been the happiest weeks of her life would now be filled with confusion and grief. Almost immediately she felt ashamed. Theo and Papa would suffer most and she must do her best for them while she could.

Go and tell him! she told herself and reluctantly set off for the house.

She found her father staring at a plate of lamb and vegetables. He held a glass of whisky and the bottle was nearby. His ruddy face had reddened unnaturally and he was breathing heavily. His knife and fork remained untouched. Without looking up he said, 'She's gone, hasn't she?'

'Yes. I'm sorry, Papa. Symes is coming up in a few minutes. I thought you'd need to question him.'

He covered his eyes with a shaking hand. 'Goddammit! What's got into the woman? Can't she see . . . ? Doesn't she know how this will look? What it will do to her? To us?' He looked up. 'Is it Cooper?'

'It looks that way. She met him at the station. It's . . . It's happened before.'

'That blackguard!'

Shocked, Nancy stared at him. 'You *knew* about it?'

'I had my suspicions but I didn't want to believe it. *Couldn't* believe it. God Almighty! I could strangle her!'

'You don't mean that, Papa.'

'Don't I? Perhaps not – but it doesn't make any sense. I thought she had everything she wanted . . .' He sighed deeply. Then he said, 'Ring for Cook. We have to eat.'

Cook came in, trying to behave as though nothing untoward was happening. She ignored the uneaten food on James's plate and went to the sideboard to carve the joint.

'There we are, Miss Nancy,' she said briskly. 'Nice bit of leg.' She put three slices of lamb on to Nancy's plate. Her smile was brittle.

'Thank you.'

They watched her remove the third place setting and hurry out. When she had gone Nancy said, 'She'll come back, Papa. She'll realise what she's done and just how much she's thrown away.'

Feeling vaguely disloyal she helped herself to carrots, beans and potatoes and discovered that she was hungry. Her father ate very little although he pushed the food around the plate. He poured himself a second glass of whisky, his expression grim.

'She wanted for nothing,' he said. 'And that damned swine, Cooper! All smiles to my face when we met at Newmarket and all the time knowing and all the time this happening behind my back. What an idiot I've been! I should have known. I should have been prepared for something like this.'

Nancy said, 'How could you have guessed? How could anybody think she would be so stupid? What can Donald Cooper offer her?'

'Don't ask!' he begged. 'Oh, Lilian!' He swallowed. 'I thought she was happy. She spent money like water and I didn't raise a finger . . . And what about her son? What am I going to tell Theo? That his mother's run off like a cheap . . . ! God Almighty!'

Nancy was now beginning to wonder how her stepmother could have been having an affair without her noticing. Had she, Nancy, been so wrapped up in her forthcoming marriage that she'd had eyes for nothing and nobody else? If only she'd been more aware of what went on around her, she might have been able to prevent this catastrophe.

She became aware that her father had stopped talking and had tossed his napkin on to the table. Before she could speak he stood up, swallowed a second glass of whisky and, with an oath, slammed his glass down on the table. For a moment their eyes met. His expression was inscrutable. Was it fear, hate or grief?

'Papa, please don't—'

But he was already striding towards the door. 'Send Symes to the study,' he told her and went out, slamming the door behind him.

'Don't do anything rash,' she finished lamely. And don't say anything you might regret, she added silently. Bad news travelled fast, especially among the racing fraternity, and she knew that as well as the impact on the family, her father would be thinking about the damage to the reputation of the stables. A personal disaster would look to some like a bad omen. Thank goodness Theo was going back to school, she thought. Maybe they need not tell him just yet of Lilian's disappearance. With any luck, if she could be persuaded to return, he need never know.

Cook came in and cleared the plates. 'I've made a syllabub,' she said unhappily. 'It won't keep.'

Nancy forced a smile. 'You know I love your syllabub,' she said. 'Bring me a large helping, Cook, and one for Nanny, too. And finish it up yourself.'

As she spooned the creamy froth into her mouth Nancy was already wondering about the following day. Without Lilian, there would be nobody to take Theo back to school as her father would be at Newmarket.

I'll have to do it, she decided. It occurred to her that if her father didn't strangle Lilian, she might be tempted to do it for him.

When Symes arrived Nancy showed him straight into the upstairs study and closed the door behind her when she left. She couldn't bring herself to listen at the door but paused at the top of the stairs for a few moments. At first she heard nothing but after a while she heard her father roar in anger and pitied the unfortunate groom. George Symes had been placed in an invidious position but the extra money must have overcome any reservations he might have had. What had he hoped? she wondered.

Perhaps that the affair would die a death and no one be any the wiser.

She was halfway down the stairs when she heard Theo calling.

'Mama! Mama-a-a!'

She hurried into his bedroom to find him sitting up in bed, wide-eyed, looking fearfully around him.

'There was a nasty big bogeyman!' he told her. 'He was chasing me and I was trying to run away and he was going to catch me and put me into a sack.'

Nancy sat on the bed and put her arms around him. 'It was a bad dream, dear. One of those silly old nightmares. There's no such thing as a bogeyman. Mama has told you that before, hasn't she?'

He nodded. 'I called Mama and she didn't come.'

'Mama's not back yet, Theo. She has to stay with her friend until the morning because . . . because she's ill and Mama is looking after her.'

'But she will take me back to school, won't she?'

'Maybe I'll come with you instead.'

His face fell. 'But she never comes. She says she will but she doesn't.'

'Of course she does. Now you snuggle down and go back to sleep and I'll leave the door open so you can see the light from the passage.'

Kissing him, she tucked him in.

She was closing the door when he called out to her. 'Is my tuckbox ready?'

'I'm sure it is.'

'Cook has made me some gingerbread men.'

'How splendid. Now settle down or we'll never wake you up in the morning.'

Downstairs in the drawing room she waited anxiously for Symes's departure. Her father would doubtless extract the rest of the story from him but what the horse owners would make of it was another matter. A scandal of such magnitude would most definitely reflect badly on the stables and that would intensify their problems. It was probably not possible to hide the truth from the owners of the horses – in fact the affair was possibly common knowledge already. The idea made her shiver. What mattered was how the owners reacted. A number of them would stand by her father, a few would adopt a 'wait and see' policy but some would take their horses elsewhere for training.

'Lilian, you thoughtless—' Only her upbringing prevented Nancy from using an unpleasant word.

And where was Lilian now? she wondered. How was she feeling? Dining with Donald Cooper, no doubt, but where? At least *he* wasn't married, she reflected. That would have made matters much worse. She wandered aimlessly around the room until she found herself staring blankly from the window. With a jolt Nancy realised that many years ago she had longed for something like this to happen. As a resentful child of ten presented with a 'wicked stepmother' she had prayed for Lilian to go away – anywhere – as long as she left Nancy and her father alone together. She had asked God to oversee the plan but He had not cooperated. Now she shook her head, appalled.

'What a vindictive little wretch I was!' she reflected.

So was this a judgement on her? She sighed as the long-forgotten memories resurfaced. No wonder Lilian had never taken to her. She had made the poor woman's life a misery in small ways but this behaviour had had the effect of turning her father against her. Or so it seemed when he was called upon to remonstrate with his daughter about her treatment of Lilian. Perhaps Lilian had been praying that Nancy would be sent away – anywhere!

The front door bell rang and for a fleeting moment Nancy thought that Lilian had returned. But that was hardly likely.

She waited as Cook made her way along the passage and then there was a knock on the door.

'It's Mr Brayde, Miss Nancy, come to see the master.'

'Ah . . . You'd better show him in here, Cook. Papa is . . . is busy on another matter.'

They avoided each other's gaze and a moment later John Brayde came into the room.

Nancy held out her hand. 'Father must have forgotten you were expected,' she began as his hand closed firmly over hers. 'If you don't mind waiting—'

She sat down and indicated that he should do the same.

'Actually, I must apologise,' he told her. 'I have called in without prior warning to ask if I could have a talk with your father tomorrow morning about—' Nancy's confusion must have showed in her face for he stopped. 'If that's not convenient then maybe the following day?'

What did he know? Nancy tried to read his expression. He was one of their horse owners – had he already heard the rumours about Lilian and Donald Cooper?

'Tomorrow isn't possible,' she said. 'My father is running your Mayberry in the two thirty at Newmarket. Aren't you going to be there?'

He shook his head. 'Unfortunately I can't attend every race. I have a farm and other business to oversee.'

'Papa will be making an early start. I'll also be away – taking Theo back to school.'

Immediately she cursed her stupidity. Now he would know that Lilian wasn't at home – if he didn't already. It occurred to her that he might know Donald Cooper. Members of the racing fraternity met regularly at the various courses.

'Back to school?' Brayde repeated. 'But isn't he at Hartleigh?'

Nancy nodded. 'This is his third term.'

'You're not driving all that way, surely?'

'No. Symes will drive us although I can manage the horses.' Suddenly the thought of spending several hours with the groom appalled her. What would they say to each other with the spectre of Lilian's defection and his implication uppermost in both their minds? She was aware of a deepening depression. Come home, Lilian, she begged silently, before matters get any worse.

'Why don't I take you?' Brayde asked. 'If your father approves, obviously. I have to see my aunt's solicitor at three only a few miles away from the school. I could drop you both off at the school and then pick you up later.'

Nancy smiled her relief. 'That would be wonderful – and Theo would be delighted. I'm sure my father won't mind.'

'Or Lawrence Wilton? Would he object?'

He's wishing he hadn't offered, thought Nancy, chastened, and hurried to reassure him. 'Lawrence will be in Dorset,' she told him. 'One of his friends has bought a house there and wants him to look it over. But I'm sure he'd be very grateful to you for your kind offer and I'd be glad of the company.'

'Then that's settled. I'll collect you just before two.'

They stood up. As they did so they both became aware of raised voices on the landing overhead and Brayde looked disconcerted. Nancy had a ghastly vision of the four of them meeting in the hallway. Instinctively she put a restraining hand on his arm.

Withdrawing it hastily, she said, 'I expect you'd like to see your horses while you're here. We could walk down to the stables together.'

Without waiting for an answer she led him through the house and out of the back door. She set off a fast pace and arrived breathless but triumphant in the stableyard where Jack Liddy, the head lad, was making his last-minute checks before her father's evening rounds. Liddy and Brayde went first to Gordie Brae where the usual concerned horse talk began and, knowing that she was no longer needed, Nancy knew she could return to the house. But she had no wish to do so. Her father would need time to calm down before he would face her. He was most likely pouring himself another large whisky. Nancy sat down on one of the mounting blocks and watched the two men. For the first time in years she envied them their passion.

Horses. She had loved them herself until she was nine when she had taken a bad fall. Her injuries had put her into hospital for months of painful surgery. Not that she blamed her mount. It was her own stupidity that had sent her into the woods, strictly against orders, where a low bough had swept her from the saddle and sent her crashing against a nearby tree trunk. She had broken a hip and her left leg and the long and uncomfortable recovery had left her with a very slight limp which showed itself when she was tired.

The two men moved across the darkening yard towards the other three horses which James Franklin trained for John Brayde. Nancy knew all about them from her father. Mayberry had thrown his lad at first gallop. Blue Boy was sound and in great form. Musket, the two-year-old colt, was under par, ignoring his food and being uncharacteristically tetchy with his lad, but her father had been unable to pinpoint any specific weakness.

John Brayde turned abruptly and crossed to her. 'We mustn't keep you out here, Miss Franklin. It turns cooler when the sun goes down. I'll finish my chat with Liddy and then I'll get off home. I look forward to tomorrow.'

There seemed nothing to keep her at the stables so Nancy reluctantly bade them both goodnight and made her way back to the house. She passed Symes, who looked sullen and didn't speak, and went in search of her father with a heavy heart.

Three

By half past one the next day everything was in hand for Theo's return to Hartleigh. Cook appeared from the kitchen carrying a small wicker hamper.

'There you are,' she told Theo. 'A tuck box to be proud of, although I say it myself!' She laughed as she opened it up and showed him the contents which were neatly packed with clean straw. 'Gingerbread men, a pot of cherry jam, your favourite carroway cake, some cheese straws and a bottle of my home-made lemonade.'

Theo thanked her, hugging the hamper, as she leaned down and ruffled his hair. Nancy smiled as he hastily smoothed it down again.

Nancy thanked Cook and fastened the straps of the small hamper which eased Theo's return to school. She thought he was happy there, but after the freedom of home it was always difficult to persuade him that he would enjoy being with his friends and learning to play better cricket. It was his oft-expressed desire to be chosen for the team when he was old enough.

John Brayde arrived in a four-wheeled dog cart drawn by a large grey to find his passengers waiting excitedly outside the front door. Nancy was surprised to find herself looking forward to the drive. The day was warm and the movement of the carriage would provide a welcome breeze. She had just seated herself and was unfurling her parasol when Cook appeared on the front step.

'It's a telephone call.'

'Is it Lawrence?' That would improve the day, thought Nancy.

'No. It's his mother.'

Nancy hesitated. To Brayde she said, 'Would you mind? Just a few minutes.'

Amelia Wilton, Nancy's future mother-in-law, could be very charming but she was very strait-laced and if she had heard anything about Lilian . . . Nancy hurried inside with a nervous flutter of anticipation. Mrs Wilton's first words put an end to any hopes she might have.

'Whatever is this I'm hearing about your stepmother?' she demanded. 'I had a telephone call ten minutes ago from a friend who insists that she saw Lilian in London yesterday with Donald Cooper. They were getting on to a train for the West Country.'

Nancy's eyes widened. 'The West Country? Good heavens!'

'Exactly! I said she must have been mistaken but she said no, she was quite certain. She said that when Lilian caught her eye she immediately alerted Donald and they hurried away to avoid a conversation with her.'

She paused but Nancy, caught off balance, had nothing ready to say and the voice went on.

'Tell me it's not true, Nancy, I simply can't believe it. "Show me a mother who would walk out on her son," I said to Harold. I know Lilian and I know there must be a rational explanation but it *looks* so bad, Nancy. "I must ring the Franklins at once," I said, "to put my mind at ease." Harold thought I should wait but I can't, Nancy. I'm so concerned – if it's true it would be so terrible for your father. For all of you. For all of us.'

Aware that her 'few minutes' were passing, Nancy said, 'Could I talk to you about this later?' She would have to tell them, she reflected, but she needed to confide in Lawrence first. She had no idea how he would react to the news except that he would be wonderfully supportive.

She said, 'Mrs Wilton, the others are waiting. I have to take Theo back to school.'

Immediately she realised her mistake.

'*You* are taking Theo back to school?'

'Yes; Lilian is . . . away.'

There was a pause during which Nancy cursed the slip.

When Mrs Wilton spoke again, her voice had risen. 'Put me on to your father at once, Nancy. I cannot rest until someone offers me some reassurance.'

'My father is on the way to Newmarket. I suggest you and I talk later. I'm sorry but I have to go.'

'Later, then, if that is the best you can do. But there is a rational explanation?'

Lilian closed her eyes. 'I'll telephone you after dinner this evening. Now please excuse me.'

As she hung up her hand was trembling. The Wiltons would not be at all pleased to know that their only son was marrying into a family tarnished by scandal. If only Lawrence was at home. She desperately needed his love and understanding.

She returned to the dog cart and climbed up with Brayde's help. They set off at once and Nancy was grateful for Theo's innocent chatter while she struggled to remain outwardly calm. From time to time she took a sideways glance at John Brayde but common sense told her that even if he knew anything about the affair, he would never raise the subject. He would certainly not discuss it in front of Theo. But what of the return journey? Suppose he asked her a direct question? Her father owed the owners' horses his undivided attention. They were worth hundreds of guineas and even more when the possible winnings were taken into account. The owners were entitled to know that James Franklin was doing his job and was not distracted by personal matters. Her father would be extremely vulnerable if Lilian's defection became common knowledge.

They reached the school after a pleasant ride, having made excellent time.

'I'll be back around five,' Brayde told her. 'Will that suit?'

Nancy nodded and she and Theo went up the steps of the mansion which served as a small private school. She had never been before, having been kept away on Sports Day by an unexpected visit to the dentist for an abscess. Theo led her proudly up the broad oak stairs and along the corridor to the dormitory which he shared with five other boys.

It was a pleasant room though sparsely furnished with six beds and a long table with drawers. Each boy had a wooden locker and Theo at once began rearranging the contents of his locker to accommodate the tuck box. What did all this cost? Nancy wondered, glancing round. Would her father still be able to afford it if he was required to make a financial settlement on Lilian? Her knowledge of such matters was extremely sketchy. Surely if Lilian had abandoned her husband and family, Donald Cooper would have to support her.

Her musings were interrupted as another small boy burst into the room to be ecstatically greeted by Theo.

'Mrs Franklin?'

Nancy became aware that a large woman in an expensive hat was holding out her hand.

'Miss Franklin,' Nancy corrected her. 'I'm Theo's sister.'

They shook hands.

'I'm Mrs Marriot. Mr Marriot had a bet on Gordie Brae last month and won. My husband said I must be sure and thank you if we met.' She smiled and lowered her voice. 'He won a nice little sum.'

'I'm afraid I can't take any of the credit,' Nancy admitted. 'I'm not connected with the running of the stables.'

'A wonderful inheritance, though, for Theo one day.'

'Indeed. We all hope he'll develop his father's passion for the job.'

'Mama! Where's my tuck box? I want to show Theo what I've brought. He's got gingerbread men.'

'Well, you've got the fudge your grandmother made for you.' Mrs Marriot rolled her eyes at Nancy. 'Why are boys so competitive? I've got two of the little monsters and they're both as bad.'

Marriot Minor was a small boy with ginger hair and a snub nose. As soon as the boys had stowed away their tuck boxes they asked permission to go out on to the playing field and, after brief goodbyes, hurried away together. Mrs Marriot went in search of her husband who was talking to the headmaster and Nancy found herself alone. She sat down on the bed, deep in thought, but was immediately interrupted by another family returning their son to his dormitory.

She went slowly downstairs, wondering if she should say anything to the headmaster about the problems at home. But, as far as she knew, Theo knew nothing of his mother's departure. In the foyer she hesitated. Was she supposed to check in with anyone? Maybe report the fact that Theo had been returned? What did Lilian do on these occasions? A glance at the clock on the wall told her that Brayde would not be returning for at least an hour so she had time to kill. She had just decided to follow the boys to the playing field when a tall bespectacled man hurried towards her with what looked like a list in his hand.

'Can I help you?' he asked.

Nancy introduced herself and they shook hands. Was it her imagination or had his expression changed?

'Theo's mother was unable to come,' she said.

'Ah!' His smile was a little thin. 'I believe the head was hoping to have a word but if she's not here . . .'

'Will I do?'

'Certainly. If you care to follow me I'll lead the way to Mr Grey's study.' He sidestepped nimbly as one of the pupils nearly collided with him. 'Boys!' he exclaimed. 'First day back they're all so frisky!'

He led Nancy back upstairs and along a different corridor. Knocking on the headmaster's door, he put his head in. 'You wanted to see Mrs Franklin, Headmaster. This is *Miss* Franklin, Theo's sister, who has come in her stead.'

Ronald Grey was in his fifties with a mane of thick white hair and very pale eyes. They sat down and he eyed Nancy unhappily over steepled fingers. She knew at once that she would not like what he had to say.

'This isn't easy,' he told her, 'but I feel it must be said for the boy's sake. It is important that the parents take part whenever possible in the school's activities – unless prevented by illness or by duties abroad. Many of the boys' parents are scattered across the Empire and return rarely to this country but that is not the case here. Theo is fortunate in having his family relatively near at hand. But visits from parents are still very important for the boy's well-being. We do make that clear when we take a new boy into the school. Letters, visits. You know what I mean.'

Nancy nodded.

'Sadly, I have to say that Theo has had less visits than any of the other boys.'

Nancy stared at him. 'Oh, but that's not true!' she exclaimed. 'His mother came to the Sports Day and again for the school play.'

It was his turn to stare. 'You are mistaken, Miss Franklin. Theo's mother did *not* attend and he was quite distraught, poor child. Parental visits are highly valued by the children, and Theo—'

'She *didn't* come? But she left—' Nancy put a hand to her mouth. Lilian had left home intending to make the visits and had returned full of details. 'I – I don't understand,' she

44

stammered. 'We assumed she had been to the school. There must be some misunderstanding . . .'

The head clasped his hands. 'It does help us to know if there are problems at home,' he said gently. 'Not that we want to pry, of course, but the boy's behaviour often changes – and not for the better. Theo is a case in point, I'm afraid. Towards the end of the term his housemaster reported that he was becoming withdrawn and his concentration weakened. I spoke to Matron and she agreed that he looked unhappy.' He leaned forward. 'Is there something we should know, Miss Franklin? For the boy's sake.'

Dismayed, Nancy stared at him. Did he *know*? Words failed her. She was trying to absorb the news that Lilian had *not* made the intended visits to the school. Had she spent the days with Donald Cooper? She felt a surge of anger as she imagined Theo waiting for her in vain.

Mr Grey said, 'I'm sorry to burden you with this, Miss Franklin, but we are very fond of Theo and want to help him if we can.'

'Has anyone said anything to him? Is anyone bullying him?'

'Bullying him? Oh no! We have very enlightened views at Hartleigh and bullying is not allowed. But apparently some of the boys tease him about his little horse.'

'Thunder? Oh yes!' Nancy smiled. 'Theo's father gave it to him on his third birthday. We're a horsey family, Mr Grey. My father hopes that Theo will inherit his love of all horseflesh!'

Mr Grey didn't even smile. 'Theo takes it everywhere, you see, and at his age . . . He'll soon be ten. Let's just say I would have expected him to have grown out of the need for a toy. Poor Theo does appear a very vulnerable child, particularly this last term. As I said, I've asked Matron to keep an eye on him.'

Nancy closed her eyes. A vulnerable child! She was

shocked by the description. He seemed happy enough at home. Cheerful and talkative. What could she say? Her father would be furious if she confided in the headmaster but Theo's happiness was at stake.

The headmaster continued, 'Matron is very good with the boys. They all talk to her freely. She's brought up a family of her own, you see. I always insist on that when I interview new staff. A childless woman will never be matron here while I'm in charge. I hoped Theo would confide in her but alas, no! Not a word. Whatever is troubling him is something he keeps to himself.'

Nancy made up her mind. 'We do have a – a slight problem,' she said carefully. 'A family problem. It involves Theo's mother but I really cannot go further than that. It isn't my place, you understand. If it cannot be resolved then I'm sure my father will write to you. I'll tell him how concerned you are.'

Afraid that he would enquire further, Nancy stood up. Reluctantly the headmaster showed her out and Nancy retreated to the foyer once more, feeling increasingly unhappy. It now appeared that Lilian had been planning to leave for some time. Nancy had been vaguely hoping that Lilian's departure had been a foolish spur of the moment decision which she would quickly regret. That was not the case.

She thought about the headmaster. Ronald Grey was obviously disappointed by what he would doubtless see as Nancy's lack of trust but she felt she had already said more than was proper. When she left him, it was with the distinct feeling that he knew more than he was admitting. Perhaps he had heard rumours . . .

She walked towards the playing field with her mind in a whirl. So where had Lilian gone on those two occasions? The answer that sprang to mind was 'somewhere with Donald Cooper' and she was sure her father would come to the same conclusion.

For half an hour she stood on the sidelines and watched the boys racing around after the ball. Theo, as one of the youngest, looked very small and helpless and the thought of his disappointment when his mother had failed to arrive made her own heart ache.

When the bell rang they all returned to the main building and Theo clung to her briefly as he prepared to go off with the other boys to wash his hands before tea.

'I'll write to you,' she promised, hugging him fiercely. 'And if you're miserable for any reason, Theo, you must tell Matron and ask her to telephone Franklins and you can talk to me or to Papa.'

'Can't I talk to Mama?'

'Or Mama,' she amended hastily. She made him promise and then watched him until he had blended into the crowd of small boys and was indistinguishable. She went outside to wait for John Brayde with a growing sense of helplessness tinged with anger.

On the way home Nancy did her best to keep up her end of the conversation but at last John Brayde asked her outright if anything was the matter.

'No!' she cried, with a vehemence that suggested otherwise. 'That is, there is but I can't talk about it.'

He nodded without comment and she felt her curt answer had been rather rude. 'It's Theo. He's having problems at school. I shall have to speak to my father . . . and stepmother.'

He nodded then glanced at her. 'Boarding school can be quite an ordeal for a sensitive child. I have to say that I loved it but not all children can cope. I had to take my daughter Lucy away from her school. She was desperately homesick and wrote such pitiful letters.'

Nancy listened with growing interest as he explained his circumstances. His wife had died soon after Lucy's birth. She was the first and only child of the marriage and was

47

being brought up by her widowed grandmother who had moved in with them.

'When Mother became ill she suggested we send Lucy to a boarding school and Lucy was very keen on the idea at first. She was nine then. Once she was there, however, she was obviously unhappy. Her letters home worried us but the head said it wasn't uncommon in the first term so we agreed to wait. We thought she'd settle down but she grew worse. She threatened to run away and then she stopped eating and began to lose weight. That was it. I brought her home and she's been taught there ever since.'

Nancy sighed. 'Life's not easy, is it,' she said. 'For the children or the parents.' Brayde gave her a quizzical look and she laughed. 'It's no easier for the sisters! Theo's only been there a couple of terms – at the same school my father went to. He's seemed to enjoy it – we've certainly had no sad letters – but the school seem to think he's suffering. We'll have to think it over carefully. Outwardly he seems a very confident boy but maybe he's hiding his fears.' She turned to him. 'Have I ever met your daughter? Has she been to Franklins with you?'

'She's come once or twice but only met your father. You never seemed to be around, though I understand you're nervous of horses since your accident. A great shame. You must miss so much.'

Nancy hid her surprise. 'I've had a lot on my mind. I expect you've heard that I'm getting married in August.'

'I had heard.'

Nancy wished he could have shown a little more enthusiasm for the idea but just then they became aware of a loud noise approaching them from behind.

Brayde said, 'Oh Lord! It's one of those damned motors!' and pulled the horse to a halt to allow it to pass. The sleek vehicle, painted cream with a brown upholstery, swept past, in a cloud of noise and fumes. The chauffeur sat in the front with a lady and gentleman behind him. The horse reared in fright and with some difficulty Brayde calmed it.

'What a frightful machine,' said Nancy, coughing. 'That poor woman must be terribly hot in all that veiling.'

'I can't see what anyone sees in them,' Brayde agreed. 'They're noisy and they're dangerous but I have a nasty feeling they're here to stay. It's called progress.' He shrugged. 'Cooper's talking about getting one, which only confirms my opinion of him.'

'Which is?'

'Too much money and too little sense.'

He urged on the horse and they moved forwards. Nancy had caught something in Brayde's tone when he spoke of Cooper.

'Is that Donald Cooper?' she asked.

'Yes. Our paths cross from time to time but I don't trust him.'

Nancy's spirits plunged once more. 'You know,' she said flatly.

'Yes. I'm sorry – about the affair. Everything.'

Nancy covered her face with her hands and breathed deeply. So much for her hopes. It was obviously common knowledge already. Or had he overheard gossip in the stableyard the night before? Abruptly she looked at him.

'So they're somewhere in the West Country.'

'Yes.'

Nancy stole a look at his face. He was concentrating on the road ahead although it was very straight with no other traffic.

Nancy felt her stomach turn over. 'But that's where . . .' She bit her lip. A disturbing thought had occurred to her. Lawrence had gone to Dorset 'to help a friend'. Cooper had run away with Lilian and they had last been seen heading in that direction.

Brayde stared straight ahead. 'He and Lawrence are friends,' he said.

Lawrence and Donald Cooper? Nancy felt frozen with shock. Lawrence had occasionally mentioned 'Don', an old school friend, but Nancy had never made the connection. Lawrence must have known about the affair and yet he'd said nothing. She said slowly, 'Does that mean that the three of them . . . That Lawrence is . . . is with Lilian?' Her mouth was dry.

'I didn't want to be the one to tell you,' Brayde said gently. 'But nor did I want you to discover later that I'd been less than straight with you.'

Nancy didn't dare speak. She was fighting down an unreasonable desire to punish him for his disclosure even though she recognised and understood his predicament. She felt humiliated but, more than that, she felt deep anger towards the man she loved most in the world.

'Oh, Lawrence!' she whispered.

Lawrence had kept all this from her. He had let this elopement take place, pretending not to know, laughing, perhaps, behind her back. Or was she being unfair? Hunched on the seat with the breeze tugging her hair, Nancy clutched the handle of her parasol with white knuckles. All other considerations fled from her mind as she tried to grapple with this fresh revelation. Lawrence, of all people! He had betrayed them. Her father would be furious if he knew – and he would find out eventually.

Brayde said, 'It's hard for you. I do understand, but these things have a way of sorting themselves out. I was in despair when Megan died. The whole world seemed upside down and every day brought new problems. But you survive. You learn to cope.'

She nodded, not trusting herself to speak.

'I'd just like to say that if I can ever help in any way, feel free to call on me. Friends are very important.'

'Thank you. You're very kind.' She spoke the trite words automatically, her mind elsewhere. She had been longing for Lawrence to return, relying on him for support. Now she didn't want to face him until she had dealt with her despair.

He smiled at her. 'Please, Miss Franklin. You must believe me. Things *will* get better,' he advised. 'Who knows? The worst may already be over.'

Fortunately neither of them could know at that moment just how wrong he was.

That evening, just before six, Nancy went in search of her father. He was in his office with Jack Liddy trying to make a provisional racing plan for the coming week. He glanced up irritably as Nancy entered so she sat down to one side and waited. She had decided to tell him all she had learned about Lilian and her whereabouts and Lawrence's involvement. Keeping information from him was pointless because it would come out later and then he would think her deceitful. She listened impatiently to the two men as they discussed the merits and demerits of each race and tried to decide which horses were ready to run.

Jack Liddy was keen to try Gold Fever at Goodwood. 'It's well turfed so reasonable going with a downhill stretch to finish and you know how Gold Fever hates to run uphill. She's a lazy devil, that one.' Thoughtfully he scratched his head with his pencil. 'Not too much competition, either. I reckon she'd be placed. *Might* win, but . . .' He shrugged.

Liddy had once been a jockey but, after a couple of bad falls, he had been persuaded by his wife to go into the training side of the sport. He had small dark eyes and Nancy had always believed he came from gipsy stock.

'But what?' her father demanded.

'The colonel wants him to run here at Epsom. He's got

51

friends coming from South Africa and he wants a day out for them.'

'I thought he wanted his horse to *win*, dammit!' James ran his fingers through his greying hair. 'Tell him it's Goodwood or nothing.'

'It's his horse, sir,' Liddy said mildly.

Her father glared. 'I know it's his horse but it's my reputation!' He shook his head. 'Let's see that list . . . Ah yes. I've promised Brayde we'll give Musket a try-out and Deakes wants to ride him here at Epsom. The left-hand course'll suit him and there'll be very little travelling beforehand. On the other hand there's bound to be a lot of runners and he's still a bit nervous.'

Liddy rubbed his chin thoughtfully. 'We could try blinkers. It worked with Carroway – which brings me to him. I was wondering . . .'

Nancy waited another ten minutes but she could see that the conversation showed no sign of ending so, catching her father's eye, she mouthed the word 'later' and left them to it.

She had no sooner set foot in the drawing room when a ring at the door sent Cook hurrying along the passage. Seeing Nancy she said crossly, 'Callers at this hour? And me halfway through the vegetables.'

Nancy sent her back to the kitchen and opened the front door to a large, matronly woman. It was Amelia Wilton. Forcing a smile and finding words of welcome, Nancy invited her in. Too late she wished she had remained in the office. It would have given her a few precious moments in which to decide how to react.

As soon as they were seated on either side of the fireplace, Amelia Wilton folded her hands in her lap. Never a good sign, thought Nancy. Not that she disliked her future mother-in-law. They were comfortable in each other's company and Nancy had no qualms about joining the Wiltons' household.

Amelia was inclined to be haughty but Harold was very approachable. When the time came Lawrence would take his place as head of the household. He helped his father run the estate and the adjoining farm and it would make no sense for the newlyweds to live anywhere else. Mannington Farm had eight bedrooms and their children would grow up in the family home.

'I'm sure you know what I've come about,' Mrs Wilton began. 'These terrible rumours. Harold didn't want me to come. Leave well alone, he said. You know Harold. Head in the sand. Always has been. But it concerns us, I told him. Our son is marrying into the family. So I came alone. I have to know the truth, Nancy. I think you owe us that much.'

Playing for time, Nancy said, 'Suppose you tell me exactly what you've heard.'

Mrs Wilton gave an exagerated sigh. 'Nothing more, I'm afraid. Have you seen, or heard from, your stepmother?'

Refusing to be cowed, Nancy gave her a straight look. 'All *we* know for sure is that Lilian went out yesterday and didn't return. She left no message and hasn't been in touch. As you can imagine, my father is distraught but we have managed to keep the facts from Theo.'

Mrs Wilton's face crumpled. 'Then we must assume they are together.'

'It looks very bad,' Nancy admitted.

'It's worse than very bad! It's disgraceful. Utterly contemptible. I'm at a loss to understand how she could do this. We've always thought her a – a rather odd choice for a man like your father, but we liked her.' She shook her head, staring into her lap to prevent Nancy from seeing the depths of her despair. 'We'd heard things about Lilian, of course. She was like a candle flame and the men fluttered round her. But young men. Men her own age. No one expected her to – to get her claws into your father.' She looked up at last. 'When they married we hoped she would settle down. Later,

53

when you and Lawrence fell in love, Harold and I decided to give her the benefit of the doubt.'

Nancy couldn't think how to respond. She would feel disloyal to her father if she agreed with their judgement but at the same time she sympathised with them.

She said, 'That was very generous of you both.' She meant it. It couldn't have been easy for them. Nancy hesitated then plunged on. 'I wonder how much Lawrence knows of the affair.'

Mrs Wilton was genuinely surprised. 'Lawrence?'

'He and Mr Cooper are friends, aren't they? Close friends from all accounts. I'm wondering whether he knew about this and said nothing. Maybe he was reluctant to betray his friend.'

A look of horror crossed Mrs Wilton's face. 'I can assure you that my son—' She stopped, frowning. In a different voice she said, 'If I thought that Lawrence knew anything about . . .' She clutched her chest. 'We can't ask him because—'

'Because he's in Dorset helping a "friend" who has just bought some property there.' Nancy nodded grimly. 'And Lilian and Mr Cooper were seen in Paddington station waiting for a train to the West Country.'

In spite of her own chaotic feelings, she was beginning to feel sympathy for the woman opposite. The Wiltons had been looking forward to their son's marriage and to the prospect of grandchildren. Now, at the eleventh hour, it seemed as though a bad fairy had arrived to cast a gloom over their happiness.

As though reading her mind, Mrs Wilton bowed her head. 'I suppose we will have to postpone the wedding,' she whispered.

Nancy gasped. 'Postpone it? Oh no! I would never agree to that – and neither would Lawrence. I'm sure he wouldn't.' Even as she uttered the words she wondered if he would stand firm. She said, 'Papa would never agree. That would be—' What would it be? she wondered. 'An admission of guilt. It would look as though Lawrence and I had something to be ashamed of. But we've done nothing wrong.'

'But surely you see how embarrassing it would be? We can't have the wedding overshadowed by this scandal. It will spoil everything.' She looked as though she was about to cry and Nancy reached across and took hold of her hand.

'We mustn't give up hope,' she said. 'Lilian might come back. She might realise her mistake. Papa would take her back, I know – for Theo's sake.'

Mrs Wilton had risen to her feet and was straightening her hat. 'Harold and I will think things over. We'll have to talk with your father. I shall pray for your stepmother to come to her senses before it's too late. In the meantime we must all put a brave face on things and say as little as possible.'

Nancy saw her to the door.

Mrs Wilton paused, her hand on Nancy's arm. 'I should have asked after your father, Nancy. I do hope he's not letting things prey on his mind. I remember when your mother died. Not to put too fine a point on it, he lost the will to live. Poor man. No one thought he'd recover from the loss.' She gave Nancy a weak smile.

'But he did!'

'Yes, he did, thank goodness. Nevertheless, this isn't easy for him. He will need all the support you can give him, Nancy. But I know you'll take care of him.'

Outside the carriage was waiting and the driver jumped down to assist his mistress. As they drove away Nancy waved, conscious of only one thing. She must see Lawrence and reassure herself that the wedding would go ahead as planned. Whatever he had done, whatever part he had played in the elopement, she would forgive him.

Dinner would be served shortly and she hurried upstairs to wash and change. She would talk to her father over the meal and together they would decide what, if anything, could be done to avert a catastrophe.

In the cottage Annie Synes faced her husband across the table, her face drawn with anxiety.

'Something's happened,' she told George. 'I can see it in your face.'

George kept his eyes on his plate. He cut a piece of mutton in half, stabbed it with his fork and pressed it into the mashed potato. Then he put it into his mouth and chewed.

'George! Answer me! Something's happened, hasn't it? Something else, I mean.'

'I'll sort something out,' he muttered.

'Sort what out? What?' She stared at him with frightened eyes. 'It's not the cottage, is it? Tell me it's not—'

'He sacked me but I'll sort something—'

'O-oh, George!' She grabbed his right hand as he reached for a piece of carrot. 'Stop this and *tell* me properly. I've a right to know. He *sacked* you?' Slowly she sat back in her chair, her eyes never leaving his face. They had lived in the cottage ever since their marriage.

He said, 'Don't take on, Annie. I've said I'll sort something out.' He put a forkful of food into his mouth and chewed.

'How you can just sit there stuffing your face . . .' Her mouth trembled.

'You'd best eat yours an' all,' he told her. 'No point in wasting good food.'

Her knife and fork had fallen from her hands and a small greasy stain spread into the checked tablecloth. Fighting tears she continued to stare at her husband, struggling to take in the awful significance of what he had told her.

At last she whispered, 'When? Why?'

'Don't ask damn fool questions, woman. You know why.'

'I mean, why blame you? It wasn't your fault. What could you do?'

He shrugged. 'Eat it while you've got it,' he said. 'We're got a month from yesterday.'

'But what . . . I mean, where . . . Oh, George! What will we do?'

He cut a thick slice of bread and wiped his plate with it. 'I'll find summat. A place like Epsom. Someone'll want a groom-cum-handyman. Come to that I can turn my hand to lots of things. Gardening.'

Nodding, Annie picked up her knife and fork. 'You can turn your hand to most things,' she agreed. But they didn't pay as well as the job he'd just lost.

'I can get work,' she reminded him.

'Not with that on the way.' He nodded towards her swelling body.

Another child on the way, she thought despairingly, and soon they'd have no home and no money.

'I can take in sewing,' she said. 'Or washing. Lots of work I can do at home.'

She was prepared to do it although it would be a struggle. Unless he *could* get a job – but that meant a good reference.

'You reckon he'll see you right about a reference?' She could hardly breathe.

'God knows.'

Which meant he wouldn't, she thought.

'I'd like to wring her blooming neck!' she muttered. 'Lilian High-and-Mighty! Thinks of nobody but herself. Walks out on her kid and gets you sacked!' She pushed the plate away.

George said, 'Eat it!'

'I can't.'

'I've worked hard to put food on the table. Eat it!'

He was right, of course. They couldn't afford to waste

anything. She put some food into her mouth and forced it down.

'Mr Franklin had no right,' she said. 'He's taking it out on you because of what she's done. It's her he should be sacking, not you.'

He sighed heavily. 'Can't sack her, can he. She's sacked herself! Stupid, selfish cow!'

'George!'

'Well, she is.' He pushed back his chair and stretched his legs. 'I'll ask around. Leave it to me, ducks. Summat'll turn up. You'll see.'

'Course it will,' she said.

But they both knew it wasn't very likely.

Four

The following day brought a change in the weather. It was still warm but the sky was overcast. It looked as grey as Nancy felt. But during breakfast a letter was delivered by hand. It came from Lilian and Nancy held her breath while her father read it. He handed it to her without a word and walked out of the dining room.

Dear James,
    I know you will never forgive me for leaving you and I do truly regret the hurt this will cause to you and the family. The initial fault is mine – I freely admit that. As you know I was vulnerable when we met and desperately wanted to fall in love with you. You persuaded me that we could make each other happy and I wanted to believe that. I was also enchanted by Franklins.

Nancy muttered disbelievingly. If Lilian had been enchanted with the stables she had hidden it very well.

I now know it was very wrong of me to marry you. I apologise for that. We both know the marriage has been a failure although I am aware that you still care deeply for me. I cannot be the sort of wife you deserve, James, and for that I am sorry. But I am still relatively

59

young and have the rest of my life to think about.
Selfish, I know, but I never pretended to be otherwise.
You married me with your eyes wide open.

Now Donald Cooper has finally offered me the sort
of life I need – excitement, travel, entertainment. I do
not blame you for denying me these things because
you are tied to Franklins and owe it your wholehearted
commitment and I knew that at the time we married.

Nancy pressed her lips together. This was not the letter of
a woman who might be persuaded to return. It had a ring
of finality that dismayed her.

I will be in touch through my lawyer in a day or two.
I know you would never allow me to have Theo and
I understand that but I hope you will allow me to see
him fairly regularly. He is my only child and despite
my actions I love him dearly although I doubt you
will believe that. Leaving Theo is the hardest thing I
have ever done.

'Then why do it?' cried Nancy. She threw down the letter
and covered her face with her hands. How could her father
bear this? The wording of the letter left him no hope at all.
Reluctantly she retrieved the letter and read on.

You will never forgive me and I cannot ask that you
do but please try to understand and think kindly of me
if you can. Lilian

Nancy reread the letter, hoping for a sing of weakness,
hoping against hope that Lilian might listen to reason but
there was no suggestion she would do so. It surprised her to

learn that early on in the relationship Lilian had been more eager than her father. Her own impression was that he had become infatuated with her and still was to some extent. Perhaps in Lilian's determination to enjoy life he had found something that was lacking in his own.

Nancy tried to consider her father dispassionately. It was true that he took pleasure from his work, from the horses and from his success. He was ambitious, even a little ruthless in his endeavours. Perhaps a little selfish, she conceded reluctantly. Lilian's pleasure in Franklins had come solely from the wins. Perfectly groomed and elegantly dressed, she had been seen to advantage at her husband's side as the owners accepted their trophies. Lilian had thrived on the admiration and reflected glory. Now, apparently, even that excitement was not enough to hold her.

But the reference to Theo – was that a good sign? she wondered. Was Lilian genuinely reluctant to take him away from his father and his inheritance or had Cooper resisted the suggestion that Theo should live with them? Did you have to choose between them? she asked the absent Lilian.

Nancy recalled Theo making a comment about 'Mr Cooper' and a kitten he'd treated cruelly. She drew in a long breath and tried to think positively. Theo didn't like Cooper and it was probably mutual. At least Theo was safe.

She needed to talk to her father but, remembering the expression on his face as he handed her the letter, she decided that could wait. Instead she went slowly upstairs to break the news to Nanny as gently as she could.

'Never coming back?' cried the old lady.

'We don't know that for certain,' said Nancy. '*She* thinks she has gone for ever but who knows? They might find that life together is not as rosy as they expected. Or Lilian might miss Theo. If Cooper has been against having Theo with them and Lilian hoped he would change his mind and he doesn't . . .' She shrugged. 'Lilian might come back.'

'That's rather a lot of "mights"!' Nanny tried to smile then her eyes filled with tears. 'Oh, that poor little lad!'

Nancy found a handkerchief for her. 'We'll make it up to him. I was hoping you would write him a long cheerful letter. He doesn't know yet, of course, but I think he would be reassured of *our* love if letters and cards arrive for him.'

Nanny brightened. 'That's a splendid idea! You always were a thoughtful child. I was wondering how to fill the morning. I've finished my magazine and I don't feel like sewing. I'll write to him right now.'

Nancy took hold of her arm and helped her over to the small writing table. She refilled the inkwell and left the old lady happily beginning her letter.

'I'll find a stamp when it's finished,' she promised.

'Thank you, dear.'

Nancy was on her way downstairs when the telephone rang in the office. Nobody seemed to be answering it. She hurried along the passage to pick it up and was greeted by the irate voice of Lady Millicent Deepny.

'What is the use of a telephone if nobody is prepared to answer it?' she demanded angrily. 'You may have time to waste but I certainly don't. I want news of Carroway. Is he running next week? Only I've had an offer for him and I thought—'

'An offer for Carroway? Oh dear!'

Nancy saw immediately that her father would be reluctant to lose him. By way of a favour to Millicent Deepny he had taken Carroway on as a very wild and badly schooled yearling. After a few months he had seen his potential and had devised a training programme for him which had brought about a great change. From a wilful horse that would bite anybody, Carroway had become calmer and more biddable but without losing his spirit. In short he had been one of James Franklin's success stories – and now his owner was prepared to sell him. That in itself was not a problem but the new owner might take the horse to another trainer.

'What do you mean, "Oh dear!"?'

Nancy regretted the careless words. 'I meant that my father will be sorry to lose him. He had great plans for him this season.'

'That may be so but it's a very good offer and I had been thinking of buying a couple of other yearlings.'

Nancy bit her lip. It wasn't her job to negotiate with owners but she was particularly reluctant to relay any news which would further depress her father. She hedged. 'I don't know where he is at the moment. Could he ring you back later?'

'No, he couldn't. I may be going out later. I'll ring again in ten minutes. That should give you plenty of time to find him.' The line went dead.

'Wretched woman!' Nancy muttered irritably. Now she would *have* to find her father.

James was in the yard, watching Cocksparrow being walked round. He looked up as Nancy approached.

'He's certainly no worse,' he said. 'Let's hope Evans was right.' To the lad he said, 'Take him along the lane towards the gallops. Don't ride him. Just a short walk. We don't want him to get stiff.'

'Or bored, sir,' the lad offered. 'This old boy's as bright as a button and he gets fidgety when he's bored.'

'Good point. So give him a few hundred yards then turn back.'

They watched him go. Her father said, 'Every horse is an "old boy" to Fred.'

Nancy took a deep breath. 'Millicent Deepny wants to talk to you. She's had an offer for Carroway.'

Her father's expression changed. 'Damn her!' He rubbed his eyes. 'Who's it from? Did she say?'

He looked tired, thought Nancy. Probably hadn't slept much last night.

She said, 'No. I didn't think to ask. It might be someone we know. Anyway, she's ringing back in about five minutes. Can you be there to take the call? I want to go over to Mannington Farm and see if Lawrence is back.'

He nodded distractedly. 'You'd better find Symes.'

'I don't want the wagonette, Papa. I'll walk across the fields. It's not going to rain.' The truth was that she needed time to decide what she was going to say to her fiancé. The revelation from John Brayde was troubling her and she had slept badly. If Lawrence was still in Dorset his parents might have heard from him. She knew she couldn't rest until she had spoken with him and hopefully understood his motives.

'Please yourself.' James took out his watch and glanced at it with irritation.

Nancy studied him anxiously. He looked thinner than she remembered and strained.

'You're not eating enough,' she told him.

'I'm fine. Don't fuss.' He put the watch away in his pocket.

'You're not unwell, are you?'

'I've just told you I'm fine! Is it any wonder if I've lost my appetite?'

'Someone has to look after you,' she began.

'I can look after myself, Nancy. I'll eat when I'm hungry and not before.'

He set off for the house, striding angrily, his shoulders stiff with resentment.

Nancy crossed her fingers and silently begged Millicent Deepny not to push her father too far. In his present mood he might retaliate and they certainly didn't want to lose any owners. Once a horse was sent to another trainer, for whatever reason, the chance of them getting the animal back was slim.

With a sigh she forced her father's problems from her mind and thought about Lawrence. Carefully hitching up her skirts she climbed over a stile which led into a large meadow. To her left, in the adjoining field, a small herd of heifers beneath an oak watched her progress. By road the journey to Lawrence's home was a good four miles but across the field it was only just over a mile and besides, Nancy wanted to be alone with her thoughts. Several things were troubling her and she wanted to consider them before confronting him. It had occurred to her that it might have been him who had brought the letter from Lilian, which certainly suggested that he was part of the conspiracy. If so, how should he deal with it? She must be loyal to her father but dreaded alienating Lawrence.

The thought of quarrelling with him over Lilian was unthinkable. She told herself she would never allow it. She would be very calm and sensible and would listen respectfully to his explanation. But the knowledge that the meeting would be fraught with problems made her apprehensive and she found her pace slowing as the Wiltons' large farmhouse came into view through the hawthorn hedge which separated the farmland from the house and gardens. She opened the white gate and closed it carefully behind her. Was Lilian ever going to return? Did she want her to return? They must hope, for Theo's sake, but Nancy thought she could bear it. Her father would have to find a kindly housekeeper or another nanny after Nancy was married. Or promote Cook and engage someone else to do the cooking. He would learn to manage as John Brayde had done when his wife died.

By the time she reached the grounds of the house proper and let herself in through the gate her thoughts were spinning and she had decided exactly nothing. It seemed, however, that someone had seen her approach for suddenly Lawrence came striding towards her, his arms outstretched in the usual welcome.

'Nancy! My dearest girl!'

'Lawrence! I've missed you so much!'

With his arms around her, Nancy closed her eyes and wished away all the difficulties but as soon as she opened them one look at Lawrence's face told her that there was no avoiding them. Guilt and apprehension were writ large in his eyes. Her own emotions were confusing but among them were anger and fear.

'Lawrence, how could you!' The words came from nowhere. She had intended to be calm and sensible. So much for planning.

'Darling, I know how it looks,' he said. 'Please don't say anything. I want to explain—'

'*I* want you to explain,' she told him, her voice sharper than intended.

With his arm around her waist he led her towards the old chestnut tree and dusted a few leaves from a wooden garden seat. As soon as they were seated he turned to kiss her again but this time she averted her face.

'You knew, didn't you?' The words were out before she could stop them. 'You knew and you said nothing! You even helped them! How could you do that to us?'

Lawrence took her hands in his and turned so he could see her eyes. 'I knew, yes. But not right away. At the beginning I thought I must be imagining it and then one day I saw them together. They didn't see me and I saw their faces and there was no denying that they were in love.'

'In love?' cried Nancy, her voice shrill. 'You call it *love* to want to persuade a woman to leave her husband and child? What sort of love is that – unless it's selfish love?' She withdrew her hands from his and clasped them together, twisting her engagement ring in an agitated way. 'I can't believe you helped them. And don't tell me Cooper is your friend. In my book that's no excuse.'

'But I didn't help them,' he protested. 'Once I realised I

tried to persuade Donald against the – the course of action he'd decided on. He simply wouldn't listen to reason. He said it was Lilian's idea. That he had never intended matters to get so out of hand but when it did he felt it would be churlish to leave her in the lurch.'

Nancy tossed her head. 'And you believed him?'

'Yes, I did.'

'Well, I don't. And I certainly don't expect you to make excuses for him. Seducing another man's wife is despicable. Oh, I know you'll say these are enlightened times and that everybody's doing it – but they shouldn't be, and that's no reason to allow Cooper to break up my father's marriage. Someone has to tell Theo his mother's abandoned him and is never coming back. Think about that, Lawrence.' She sat back, increasing the distance between them. 'And you went to Dorset to their cosy little love nest to be with them! That's unforgivable, Lawrence, and in your heart you—'

He held up a hand to stop her. 'I went to Dorset to help them move in but I intended to make a final plea for them to end the affair.'

'And did you ask them?'

'I tried but they wouldn't listen.'

'Perhaps you didn't try hard enough!'

'They were so excited and happy . . .' He looked at her miserably. 'I thought of how happy we were going to be when we married and—'

'When! That's a big question now, isn't it. Our family is thrown into confusion and it's partly your fault. Didn't you see, Lawrence, how it would harm our prospects? It's unforgivable!'

'I couldn't bear to spoil their happiness.'

'They don't deserve to be happy at someone else's expense.'

He sat back and stared up at the sky, silenced by her hostility.

'Papa isn't eating. He's drinking instead. He looks ill. Oh,

Lawrence, if you could only see what this is doing to him you wouldn't defend them!'

'I don't defend them. I know they did wrong and I tried to persuade them, Nancy. I wish I could convince you of that.'

Nancy stared at him. With all her heart she longed to believe him but somehow she remained unconvinced. 'But when you knew Cooper had bought the house down there, you must have guessed who was going to live in it. You've known all along what was happening and you didn't even warn us.'

'How could I come to your father to tell him his wife was being unfaithful? Think, Nancy. He would have hated me for it. I couldn't risk that. I want to marry his daughter, remember.'

Nancy took a deep breath, trying to retain her composure. 'But everybody must have known! They must all have been laughing at us!'

'I know how hard it is for you—'

'No, you don't! I had to talk to Theo's headmaster and make excuses for Lilian. Can you imagine how awful that was?'

'*You* took Theo back to school?'

'Papa was racing.'

'That was a long journey.'

'John Brayde took us. He was going that way and offered to drive us.'

Lawrence looked displeased at this and Nancy took a little comfort from the fact. Was he jealous?

'Brayde? I've never liked the fellow.'

'Really? I can't think why not. I thought him very generous. He needn't have bothered and he was very understanding. He's brought up his daughter single-handed since his wife died.'

'You mean I'm *not* understanding?'

68

She could see he'd been stung by her tone but she was unrepentant. 'I didn't say that. You're twisting my words. I just wondered why you don't like him.'

'Why? Because one of his horses lost me a lot of money a few years ago, that's why! Silverman should have won and I had a tidy packet on him. It was neck and neck but Brayde's jockey was on Gordie Brae and he bumped Silverman's jockey. Deliberately put him off his stride. Gordie Brae won by a nose.'

Baffled, she sought for an explanation. 'Wasn't there an enquiry? There usually is.'

He rolled his eyes. 'There was but they found no cause to disqualify the result.'

'Then how can you hold it against John Brayde – or his jockey?'

'Because I know what I saw.'

'Aren't you ever mistaken? Most people are. It all happens so quickly in the heat of a race.'

'For heaven's sake, Nancy! I don't expect you to understand.'

'Because I'm a woman? Don't you dare say it!'

'I wasn't going to.' His mouth tightened.

'You were! You meant that because I'm a mere woman I can't be expected to have any intelligence.' She felt herself stiffen.

'Nancy! Please . . . You're being ridiculous.'

'How charming!'

'Darling! We must stop this. I don't want to argue with you over Brayde. He gave you a lift. Very kind of him. Now let's forget it.'

He had turned away from her and was staring angrily across the lawn. Nancy folded her arms across her chest. She felt annoyed and resentful, cheated by an unkind fate. She was quarrelling with the man she loved most in the world and had been driven to it by circumstances over which she had no control. She knew they ought to forget it so why was she still annoyed with him? It was the first time she had felt ambivalent towards him and it troubled her more than she wanted to admit.

She said, 'Your mother came round while you were away. She seems to think we should delay the wedding. I said I couldn't agree to that. My dress is nearly finished and everything is booked. I want us to be married as planned.' I want to walk away from all the heartache, she thought guiltily, and start my new life. She longed to tell Lawrence how she felt but that would make her sound as selfish as Lilian.

She waited for Lawrence to agree but instead his expression changed.

'We should talk about that,' he said. 'She mentioned it to me and I have to say I think Mother's right, Nancy. I don't want us to marry in a soured atmosphere. I want everything to be perfect, the way it was.'

'You know it never can. We can't turn back the clock.'

He regarded her unhappily. 'A couple of months won't make that much difference, surely. It's not as if we can't change the date. They haven't called the banns yet.'

Nancy felt as though he'd slapped her. She couldn't believe that he could accept his mother's suggestion so calmly.

'So when will you consider it a suitable time?' she asked, her heart thumping. 'When – and if – Lilian returns?'

'That would be ideal.'

'And if she doesn't? How long do you plan to wait? If I agree to put it off for two months, what then? You might delay it further – if your mother thinks it best.' She knew she sounded shrewish but at that moment she almost hated him. After all the humiliations of Lilian's departure, she was now being betrayed by Lawrence.

'I thought you loved me,' she said, aware that a note

of desperation was creeping into her voice. 'I thought you couldn't wait until we were man and wife. That's what you told me a few days ago. Now suddenly you are able to wait. You *want* to wait.' More than anything she wanted him to put his arms around her, kiss her and hold her safe. Somehow, however, there seemed to be a gulf growing between them that they could not overcome.

'I thought *you'd* want to wait,' he said. 'Marrying in the public eye with a scandal hanging over you . . .'

'Over *me*?' Stung by the careless words, Nancy sprang to her feet. 'Over *me*? What have I done? It's not my scandal, Lawrence, and it's cruel of you to suggest it!'

He stood, trying to take hold of her hand. 'Listen to me, Nancy!'

She shook off his hand. 'No, I won't,' she cried, close to tears. 'You listen to me. If you haven't the courage or loyalty to stand by me when things get difficult then maybe you don't want me enough. Maybe you *should* listen to your mother. Perhaps she knows best. Perhaps we should end this engagement – or would that be one scandal too many?'

Impulsively she snatched at her engagement ring but it was a snug fit and wouldn't move. Frustrated, she turned from him and, gathering up her skirts, began to run back towards the gate. After a moment he began to run after her but she ignored his demands that she stop. By the time she reached the gate and glanced back she saw that he had already relinquished the chase and she didn't know whether to be glad or sorry. Her eyes were blurred with tears as she closed the gate behind her and retraced her steps through the long grass. But her tears were of anger. If he didn't want her he had only to say so. She would send back the ring with a scathing letter that would set his mother's ears tingling. She desperately wanted to blame Amelia Wilton but she knew that Lawrence could have rejected her idea.

'You're finding me an ambarrassment,' she muttered.

71

'Well then, be rid of me.' As she neared the house she forced back the tears that threatened. In spite of her brave words her heart ached with misery. Lawrence meant everything in the world to her and the thought of losing him was unbearable.

She returned to the house longing for the privacy of her bedroom but as soon as she set foot on the first stair, Cook appeared from the kitchen looking none too happy.

'What is it?' Nancy asked wearily.

'It's all the extra work, Miss Nancy. Since the mistress has been away. What I mean is, if it's just a day or two I could muddle through but when is she coming back? I can't be doing with it all on my own. It's too much what with poor old Nanny to keep an eye on and—' She shrugged. 'I'm not getting any younger and I could do with a spare pair of hands in the kitchen.'

Nancy regarded her wearily. Another problem. 'I can do more for Nanny,' she began but Cook shook her head.

'What I'd really like is someone to help with the cooking, laying the tables and so on. Not that I'm one to complain but a body can only do so much. I was wondering about Mrs Symes.'

'Oh no! I don't think so.' Surely Cook knew by now that her father had sacked George Symes. 'They won't be staying, I'm afraid. And I don't think my stepmother will be coming back.'

Cook's eyes widened. 'Not ever?'

Nancy hesitated then decided she might as well break the news. It would reach Cook's ears eventually. 'Mrs Franklin has left my father . . . for someone else. We don't expect her to return.'

Her eyes widened. 'Oh, but— Oh!' A hand went up to her mouth. 'What about Master Theo? We shall miss him something dreadful!'

'Theo will stay with us. He doesn't know yet. As for the

work – I'll talk to my father about some help for you. Maybe a girl from the village would come up for a few hours a day.' She smiled. 'It's all very sad but we'll get through it somehow. As for tonight's meal—'

'I'll be making a shepherd's pie with the rest of the joint and Mr Symes will find me some vegetables like he usually does.' She frowned. 'They're going, you say? Bit sudden, isn't it? They might have let you know earlier.'

'It wasn't like that, Cook. Papa has given Mr Symes notice. He – that is, Mr Symes – has behaved very badly towards us, and my father . . .' To her annoyance she heard her voice shake.

'Behaved badly? But what's he done?'

Suddenly Nancy couldn't put it all into words. 'He's been disloyal. I don't want to go into details.'

Cook said quickly, 'Well, I'm sure it's none of my business, Miss Nancy. But the cottage? I mean, where will they go?'

'That's not your concern, Cook.' Shaken by her encounter with Lawrence, Nancy needed to be alone with her thoughts – but apparently that was going to be a luxury from now on. She drew a deep breath, aiming at a semblance of composure.

Cook had reddened, mortified by the rebuke. She said stiffly, 'Well, please tell your pa how sorry I am about his wife.'

'Thank you. It's all very sad.'

Cook glanced about her as though seeking an escape from the situation. 'Well, I'd best get back to the kitchen.'

Nancy clung to the banisters. It seemed that everything that could go wrong would do so. She blinked rapidly to keep back tears of helplessness. She must speak to her father before she forgot Cook's request.

She found him in the stableyard with Millicent Deepny and a man Nancy didn't recognise. Presumably this was the potential buyer. They were grouped around Carroway who had been been brought out of his stall by his lad. Her father glanced up at Nancy's arrival and she saw from his expression that matters were not going the way he had hoped. This was definitely not the time to mention Cook's request. It was a time to support her father, who looked distinctly annoyed.

Millicent Deepny said, 'Good morning, Miss Franklin,' in a frosty tone. She was a handsome woman who spent a great deal of money buying clothes that disguised her more than ample figure. She waved a hand by way of introduction. 'Mr Cecil Travers, Miss Franklin.'

The stranger was a tall thin man with a moustache and very pale blue eyes. He gave a little bow in Nancy's direction but his smile lacked warmth.

Pretending not to notice the frosty atmosphere, Nancy said, 'A pleasure, Mr Travers. I see you're admiring Carroway. He's one of our favourites. My father has wrought a transformation with him. I know he's expecting great things from him.' She wondered how far a little charm would go and smiled.

Travers said, 'A lovely animal, I agree. Beautiful lines. If I buy him he'll be my first and I'll hope to buy a second at some time. I've had a little luck recently with my overseas investments and thought, Why not? My brother races and he's been encouraging me to "invest in horseflesh" as he puts it.' He smiled. 'So what do you think, Miss Franklin? Would you buy Carroway if you were me?'

Nancy thought quickly. 'It depends on whether or not you are planning to move him. He's very settled here and quite promising. Horses hate change, you know.'

Nancy was aware that Millicent Deepny's expression was growing colder by the minute.

Travers looked thoughtful. 'The point is, we live near Brighton and my brother is very impressed with his trainer.

74

A Sussex family called Lewis. Two brothers, in fact. Makes more sense.'

Nancy, recognising panic in her father's eyes, gave a light shrug. 'I think it would be a shame to move him at this time, Mr Travers. Carroway's likely to do very well this season but a change of environment might be rather disruptive for him. It might well throw him off his stride, so to speak. Might ruin his chances.'

Millicent Deepny glared at her. 'What nonsense! Horses exchange hands all the time. If he buys the horse he can do whatever he likes with it.'

Nancy pretended not to have heard and went on smoothly, 'If Carroway has a successful season his reputation would be greatly enhanced. Buy him by all means but why not leave him with us at least for the season? You could make a decision about moving him later.'

Her father said, 'That's not a bad idea, Nancy.'

Millicent Deepny looked relieved and Nancy crossed her fingers. With her other hand she reached up and patted the horse's soft nose. 'He's happy here. It seems a shame to upset him for no good reason.'

Travers looked from one to the other and nodded slowly.

Her father said, 'If you were happy with our training systems I'd be willing to help you buy another horse. I'm an old hand at the Sales. We could spend a couple of days in Doncaster together.'

This offer seemed to settle matters. Everyone was pleased that the horse would be sold to Travers but would remain at Franklins for at least a few months. Nancy was gratified to see her father relax a little. He deserved some good news, she reflected, and was glad she had been able to help. She was also delighted that anyone had found her advice worthwhile. It was a heady feeling which gave her confidence when she needed it most.

Later that evening she asked her father about the cook's request for extra help and he told her to see to it.

'I've too much on my plate,' he explained. 'Find someone biddable and pay her the going rate.'

Nancy wanted to confide in him about her quarrel with Lawrence but on reflection decided not to burden him with any more problems. She noticed that he drank several glasses of port after the meal and hoped that alcohol wasn't going to be his answer to his difficulties. Drink had been the downfall of her paternal grandfather and she didn't think the Franklins needed another disaster.

More than anything Nancy missed the security that Lawrence's love had given her. Without it she felt lonely and strangely unsubstantial, as though a part of her was missing, and before she settled to sleep that night she prayed that their differences would soon be settled. Perhaps she should write to Lawrence and try to make the peace between them.

'First thing in the morning,' she promised herself and slipped into sleep feeling slightly more hopeful.

Five

That same night Theo lay in bed in his dormitory thinking about his home and in particular about the young goat that his father had promised as a companion for Bay Lover. Button. It was a wonderful name. Tomorrow was Wednesday and that was letter-writing day. He would write to his mother and ask her about the goat and remind her that his name would be Button and that he had told Marriot Minor about it and he was really jealous. Marriot's father and mother lived in a flat in London and could never have a goat because there was no grass.

He turned on to his right side and tried to get to sleep but remained wide awake. Around him most of the other boys slept and some made soft snuffling noises which Theo thought was silly. He hoped he didn't make noises like that. The boy in the next bed was called Betts. He was crying but he was new and that was understandable. Theo thought that maybe tomorrow he would give Betts one of his gingerbread men.

At the far end of the room an older boy slept. He was eleven and a prefect. He was supposed to look after the younger boys and his name was Tompson and they all called him Tommy. Theo thought it very grand to have a nickname and had often thought of telling his friends to call him Frankie but when he had talked to his mother about it she had told him not to be silly.

'You have a name already,' she had told him. 'Theo

is perfectly acceptable. Frankie sounds like a name for a bookie.'

Theo remembered how sharply she had spoken – but then she often spoke like that when Mr Cooper was there. He frowned into the darkness. Mr Cooper was a horrible man. One day he had picked up Mrs Symes's kitten by its tail and laughed when it squealed.

Unable to sleep Theo sat up in bed and looked round the room. The lights were off but moonlight filtered in through the windows. As he looked he saw Tommy get out of bed. He wore blue silk pyjamas which Theo envied. His own were red and white striped cotton and he hated them.

Tommy fumbled in his bedside locker and then made his way softly along the room towards Theo.

He stopped when he reached his bed and tossed something on to the counterpane.

'There you are, Franklin,' he whispered. 'Don't tell the others.'

Astonished, Theo picked up a bar of chocolate.

'Thank you,' he replied, puzzled by the gesture. 'But why?'

Tommy stood beside the bed, resplendent in his silk pyjamas. 'My mother said to be specially nice to you. It's because of your mother.'

Theo stared at him, unable to understand why Tommy's mother wanted him to have a bar of chocolate.

'But why?' he repeated.

'You know – because of what's happened. My mother said it was a wicked thing to do and my father said, "What can you expect? Chalk and cheese."'

Theo frowned. Had his mother done something wicked? He tried to think of some wicked things. Had she stolen something? Or stabbed somebody? She might have told a whopping lie but he didn't think so. 'I don't believe you,' he said. 'Mama doesn't do wicked things.'

'Oh Lord!' Tommy sat down on the side of the bed. 'Don't say they haven't told you.'

'Haven't told me what?' The chocolate bar felt cool and slim in his small hand. Theo wondered if he should eat a piece and offer some to Tommy. 'Is it for now?'

Tommy shrugged. 'Whenever you feel like it. It's to cheer you up . . . You really don't know?'

'I'm not allowed to eat in bed.'

'Then save it for tomorrow. I'll tell my mother I gave it to you. She's run away and left you.'

'Who has? Your mother?'

The new boy in the next bed sat up. He was still crying and was wiping his eyes on the sheet. Tommy turned to him. 'For heaven's sake stop snivelling, Betts. You'll get used to it. We all do. And blow your nose.'

Betts went on sniffing.

Theo said, 'Why has your mother run away?'

Tommy said, 'Not my mother, stupid. Yours. She doesn't love your father any more so she's run away with another man so now you haven't got a mother and that's why my mother is sorry for you. I thought you knew. Everybody else knows.'

Theo was astonished. He knew it couldn't be true because his mother would never do such a thing but if he said so he would have to give back the chocolate bar.

Tommy turned back to Betts. 'Where's your handker-chief? I told you to blow your nose.'

'I w-want to go h-home.'

'Well, you can't, can you. You think you've got troubles? You should be in Franklin's shoes!' He stood up. 'Anyway, both of you, get off to sleep.'

Theo nodded. In silence he watched Tommy go back to his own bed. Then, greatly daring, he tore open the chocolate, gave some to Betts and had some himself.

Before he drifted into sleep he decided that in the morning he would ask Matron about his mother.

*   *   *

Next morning Nancy woke from a restless sleep with a deep feeling of gloom. She washed and dressed early and went down to breakfast, hoping to avoid her father. Depression was making him bad-tempered and although she understood his frustration, she was finding it hard to remain cheerful. Seeing that he wasn't in the breakfast room and that the table was undisturbed, she assumed he had gone to the gallops and might eat later. After a quick meal of toast and honey she hurried to the kitchen to discuss the day's menus and then went upstairs to collect Nanny's breakfast tray.

'How is your father coping?' the old lady asked as she struggled into a sitting position against the pillows.

'He's suffering,' Nancy admitted. 'I think he'll have a dreadful hangover this morning.'

'Oh dear!' Nanny looked at her anxiously. 'Do keep an eye on him, dear. Call the doctor in if you're at all worried.'

'The doctor? He's not ill, Nanny. He's drinking too much, that's all.'

Nanny looked at her tray, which was set as usual with a lace cloth, silver teapot, sugar bowl and milk jug.

Nancy said, 'Scrambled egg and bacon under the cover.'

'You're all so good to me, dear. I sometimes wonder . . .'

Nancy broke in quickly. 'Of course you deserve it. We all need to be spoilt a little. I hope someone looks after me when I'm your age.'

'Oh, but of course they will! You'll have your Mr Wilton. And he'll have you.' She smiled at the rosy picture this conjured up. 'Now you leave me to my breakfast, Nancy. I'm sure you've got things to do.'

Nancy lifted the cover from the bacon and eggs and set it on the bedside table. 'I've got the dressmaker coming this afternoon with the skirt and bodice together. I'll come up and show you.'

She was halfway to the door when Nanny called to her. 'Watch out for your father, Nancy. He's . . . he's not as strong as you might expect.'

Not as strong? An odd choice of words, she thought as she closed the door behind her. But she remained uneasy. She had always thought of her father as hale and hearty – he certainly looked fit. Was there something she didn't know? Making up her mind to ask Nanny later what she meant, Nancy made an effort to concentrate on the matter in hand – her wedding gown and her wedding. Suppose it were to be delayed. Nancy was under no delusions. The fat *would* be in the fire because Mrs Bailey's tongue would wag and all the town would know. Epsom would be buzzing with the news and it would spread like the proverbial bush fire. If it were to be *cancelled* . . . She couldn't even consider such a disaster. For the first time Nancy faced the fact that Lilian might have spoilt not only her own life but Nancy's as well. The thought was like a blow to the heart and she paused halfway down the stairs and leaned against the banisters while she thrust the unwelcome idea from her mind. Did she really want to risk losing Lawrence? She had been too hasty, she reflected, and had overreacted. She must write to Lawrence at once to say how sorry she was for the argument they had had. Surely he would understand the strain she was under.

As she crossed the hall she was surprised to see Jack Liddy waiting there, his trilby hat clutched in his hands.

'I was looking for a word with your father, Miss Nancy.'

She frowned. 'Isn't he at the stables?'

'No, miss. He didn't turn up for the gallops either. I thought maybe he was ill.'

Nancy's gloom became unease. 'I don't know where he is. He wasn't at breakfast. Will you wait a moment while I find him?'

'Righto, miss.'

Nancy hurried into the office which was empty and then into the kitchen. Cook hadn't seen him and Nancy rushed up the stairs to his bedroom and tapped on the door. When no one answered, she went in. Her father lay sprawled across the bed in the clothes he had worn to dinner the previous night. Her heart began to pound. To the best of her knowledge, this was the first time her father had ever missed the gallops. Morning exercise was the best time a trainer had to assess the success or otherwise of his training programme. She knew how much her father enjoyed watching his horses cantering past in the early morning air. The fact that he had missed it sent a shock wave through her.

'Papa! Wake up!' She approached the bed fearfully and, seeing how pale he was, wondered if he might be ill. Reaching for his shoulder she shook him gently and he groaned. 'Papa! Are you sick?'

He finally opened his eyes and then covered them with his hand to keep out the light. 'What's up?' he muttered. 'What time is it?'

'It's after nine,' she told him. 'You missed morning exercise and Mr Liddy wants to speak to you. He's downstairs.' She didn't ask again whether he was ill. The smell of whisky was still on his breath. 'You have to get up, Papa, and wash and shave. What shall I say to Mr Liddy?'

He tried to sit up and groaned. 'God Almighty! My bloody head!' he muttered thickly. 'Get Cook to brew up some strong coffee – and tell Liddy I'll be down shortly.' He sat up at last and swung his legs over the edge of the bed. Embarrassed by seeing him in such a state Nancy glanced away, taking in the room to which Lilian had added many small, feminine touches – flowery wallpaper, an ornate display of silk poppies. Among these delicate items her father looked incongruous.

Nancy had never seen her father unshaven and had certainly never seen him recovering from a drinking bout.

It was a good thing Lilian couldn't see him in this state, she reflected – but then, if Lilian had still been around her father would not *be* in this state.

'I'll send up another jug of hot water,' she said, preparing to leave the room. 'You won't go back to sleep again, will you, Papa?'

He raised his head cautiously. 'Just get out and leave me to it!'

Nancy made her way downstairs to find Liddy still twirling his hat.

'My father will join you in the stables in about fifteen minutes,' she told him. 'He sends his apologies. It's very unusual for Papa to oversleep. You'll have to forgive him.'

She watched him go then made her way to the morning room and opened up the writing desk. Taking a sheet of notepaper she tried to think how best to express herself. Something told her that this letter might be important. If Lawrence was really angry with her . . . If he had confided in his mother . . .

My dearest Lawrence,
How foolish of us to part yesterday on bad terms. Neither of us wished it, I am certain. If I hurt you in any way by my words I ask you to forgive me.

It may be difficult for you to understand what a strain I am under, what with grief for my father and for Theo as well as dismay at my own predicament and anxieties about Franklins. I ran from you with tears in my eyes and an ache in my heart and I think you felt something similar . . .

Nancy reread her words and wondered whether she was too willing to shoulder the blame. Sighing, she pursed her lips thoughtfully but could see no way to rephrase the letter. She went on:

83

Do please let us meet again before long and with memories of our quarrel behind us. Our love for each other should not be blown about by unkind winds of fate. We must cling on to what we have and ensure our future happiness. Once your parents realise how much we need each other I'm sure all talk of delays will vanish. Your devoted Nancy.

She added a kiss and folded the letter before she could change her mind. Slipping it into an envelope she decided to send Symes across the fields to deliver it by hand.

An hour later she had given Symes the letter and his instructions. It occurred to her that she should check up on her father and make sure that he had met up with Liddy.

She found them both in the stableyard, discussing Gold Fever, one of Colonel Harding's fillies. Relieved, she saw that her father looked no worse for his over-indulgence. He had shaved and there was some colour in his face.

Jack Liddy was talking while Nancy's father ran his hand down each of the horse's legs in turn.

'The way I see it, Guvnor, she may have done her best. She struggled, those last two races last year. Deakes was very unhappy with her.'

Her father straightened up, still unaware of her presence. 'But she looked as good as any other three-year-old. Lovely win at Colchester.' He sighed, patting Gold Fever's sleek black neck. She immediately tossed her head so that her mane fluttered in the gusting breeze. 'What does the colonel think? Any clues?'

Liddy shrugged. 'Hard to say. He did mention selling her if she's outdone herself. Some horses reach their peak at three years old. Hard to say. We could give her one more race if we keep away from the serious opposition.'

It was always 'hard to say', thought Nancy. Horses were constantly delighting or disappointing their owners

84

and trainers. They were temperamental creatures, always on or off form, teetering on the edge of success or failure.

Her father frowned. 'Might be better to let her go as a brood mare before her performance dips. I'll try and get hold of the colonel this evening.'

Liddy said, 'I'd like you to take a look at Musket. Bit sparky this morning. Twitchy, his lad reckoned. Had him off twice. Once he was spooked by a magpie—'

James saw Nancy and held up a hand. Liddy waited.

Nancy said quickly, 'I've talked to Cook and she knows a girl who might be willing to come in. Someone who would start immediately. I'll be speaking to her after the vicar's visit.'

'The vicar? What the blazes does he—'

'The wedding, Papa!'

'Oh! Right then.'

Seconds later the two men had their heads together and another lad was leading out two-year-old Musket. Nancy remembered him as a gawky yearling with no name. He was simply called the Lansbury colt because that was the name of his sire. Nancy had watched him grow from a wide-eyed, long-legged foal into something approaching a horse. She had watched as the first bit was slipped into his mouth and the first roll of padding was placed on his back. At that stage he had been what Liddy called 'larky' which might or might not have been a good sign.

As Nancy reached the house, the vicar's buggy was already outside the front door and she greeted him a trifle nervously. What had he heard, if anything? She hoped he wasn't going to offer condolences because she didn't think she could take too much kindness.

Reverend Blakely was a short man with a monklike fringe of grey hair around his ears. He was nearing seventy and had spent most of his working life in or near Epsom. He had christened Nancy and Theo and had married James and

Lilian. Now he sprang from the buggy with unexpected ease and hurried to take Nancy's hand. By his cheerful greeting, she suspected that he knew nothing of the rumours. As she led him into the drawing room she wished she had had time to prepare a little speech of explanation. Now she would have to improvise.

The vicar was full of smiles and explained that before the wedding he wanted to speak to them both about the expectations of marriage and the meaning of their vows. It soon became clear that the vicar was going to be the last person in Epsom to hear about Lilian. Nancy missed an early chance to confess to the situation and then, in the face of the man's enthusiasm, found it increasingly difficult.

'We shall pray for fine weather, my dear, and I'm sure God will smile on you.' He beamed at her. 'Your father must be very proud. His only daughter marrying a man he heartily approves of. The Wiltons are a charming family and they have been very generous to our little church. You will recall that we had a leak in the roof. Harold Wilton was largely instrumental in making the repairs possible. And I christened young Lawrence!' He sighed happily. 'A love match and very suitable to boot! What more can a fond father ask, eh?'

Nancy didn't enlighten him. If the wedding had to be postponed he might well ask her why she had failed to trust him with the facts. She would have to have an excuse ready. Perhaps she would pretend that she thought he must know and was trying to spare her any embarrassment.

They agreed the banns although Nancy insisted that he check with the Wiltons before he fixed the date officially in his records.

'The list of invitations is almost complete,' she told him.

'Good, good.'

'And I shall order the flowers next month. Have I forgotten anything?'

'The bells, of course,' he said. 'I have booked them for you, as your stepmother requested. Also the choir.'

As the conversation proceeded, Nancy's discomfiture deepened. Without Lilian, she was unsure what remained for her to arrange. The bridesmaids were two of Lawrence's young cousins. She knew their dresses were being made by their mother. But what about ushers? And what had Lilian said about caterers? There was also the marquee to consider. Had Lilian ordered it already?

'And we'll see you all next Sunday, I trust?' said the Reverend Blakely, as he prepared to leave.

'All of us? Ah . . .' She forced a smile. 'My stepmother may not be able to attend but – but she'll be there if at all possible.'

'Not indisposed, I hope.' He paused on the doorstep.

'No . . . Family commitments. Nothing to worry about.'

'Good. Good.'

As he touched his whip to the horse, Nancy felt a weight settle on her shoulders. Family commitments?

'Too many half-truths and evasions!' she muttered. She wasn't used to deceptions.

As she closed the door, she knew that in her present frame of mind the last thing she wanted to do was try on her wedding dress. Impulsively she lifted the telephone and gave the operator the dressmaker's number. When Mrs Bailey answered Nancy pleaded a sick headache and asked her to come the following day instead. As she replaced the receiver she had a sudden thought. Would etiquette demand that they invite Lilian to the wedding?

'Certianly not!' was her instinctive response. Lilian's presence would set the tongues wagging in earnest, she thought. A bad fairy at the feast. But wouldn't Theo want her to be present? Would her father want to see her? He had never said he didn't love her and probably still did. He might be praying that she would return – for Theo's sake if not for

87

his own. Nancy sighed. There were still a few weeks to go and the future was still uncertain.

'But she's not my mother. I don't need her.'

The thought of her stepmother's treachery was still a fresh wound but Nancy knew she must think about the others. If her father wished it she would invite Lilian but if the choice was hers alone, she would never be welcome at Franklins again.

'Never!' she said aloud. But even as the word rang in her ears, she knew she was being selfish. Lilian was Theo's mother and he needed her. Nothing could alter that.

That night the ringing of the telephone woke Nancy and she struggled into her dressing gown. A glance at the clock showed her it was half past eleven. She ran to her father's room and called to him but he didn't answer. She tried to open the door and discovered that it was locked.

She rushed down the stairs, nearly falling in her haste.

'Hullo. Franklins. Nancy speaking.'

For a moment there was silence.

Then a man's voice said, 'I want a word with your father.'

'You can give me a message.'

'She's coming to see you tomorrow morning with her solicitor. I thought you should know.'

Nancy said, 'What are you talking about? I think you may have the wrong number.'

'Lilian. She'll be there about ten with her solicitor.'

Light dawned at last. 'Is that Donald Cooper?'

'Right first time.'

Nancy thought fast. 'It may not be convenient.'

'Better make it convenient. She wants the boy.'

'No!' Nancy shouted. 'Tell her that's not possible. Theo belongs with his father. Put her on the line, please.'

'I can't do that. She's sleeping.'

'Then wake her up! I need—'

The line went dead. Nancy hung up, her throat tight with fear. Lilian was coming to Franklins with a solicitor. What did that mean? Had she any legal right to take her son away? Wrapping her dressing gown more closely around her she made her way into the sitting room and collapsed into the sofa. No point in trying to rouse her father now. He had probably been drinking again. She would tell him in the morning. But what should they do? Presumably they should contact their own solicitor.

She thought about Donald Cooper. He was obviously acting without Lilian's consent or knowledge. So had they fallen out so soon? Nancy disliked the very thought of Cooper but at least he had given them a chance. They had been forewarned of Lilian's intentions.

Wide awake, her thoughts chaotic, Nancy busied herself in the kitchen making herself a cup of hot milk. She added two spoonfuls of sugar and stirred it thoughtfully. Once back in her bedroom she climbed into bed and drank it slowly as she tried to see a way through the maze of problems that had beset the family. If Lilian somehow gained control of Theo against Cooper's wishes the boy would have a miserable time of it. By the time the mug was empty she was no wiser and settled down beneath the sheets without much hope of sleep.

The following morning Lilian arrived promptly at ten o'clock, accompanied by an elderly man who wore spectacles and carried a cane. When the front door bell rang Nancy, perched on a stool, was slowly turning while Mrs Bailey adjusted the hem of her skirt. It hung straight to the ankles with only a few slender darts to shape it over the hips.

Cook sent the new girl to the front door to let the visitors in but although Nancy listened, she heard very little. She wished that she had thought to cancel Mrs

Bailey's visit completely. It wouldn't take the dressmaker long to broadcast the news of Lilian's visit and it would certainly be more newsworthy than the postman's accident or the choirmaster's argument with the organist.

Mrs Bailey, who had previously made no reference to Lilian, had obviously recognised her voice and now gave Nancy a questioning look.

Nancy drew a deep breath. 'Yes. It's Mrs Franklin. I expect you've heard what happened.'

Mrs Bailey sat back on her heels. 'That's as straight as I can get it.' She removed the pins from her mouth. 'Well, I must admit I was told things. Mrs Marden was full of it. I said, "Never in a million years!" but she was adamant. All done. You can step down now.'

Nancy stepped down from the stool and put a hand to her back.

'Bit stiff?'

'A little.'

Mrs Bailey slipped in a couple more pins and said, 'Such a dreadful thing to happen! I said, "Surely not!" You can slip it off if you like. I've finished.'

Nancy allowed the creamy satin to slide to her ankles and stepped carefully out of it.

'You're going to look wonderful!' The dressmaker gathered up the material and carried it to the table. 'Have you decided on the bouquet?'

'I've hardly had time to think about it,' Nancy confessed. 'Since Mrs Franklin left it's been so chaotic . . .'

'You poor thing!' Mrs Bailey's distress was genuine. 'You ought to be so happy and now all this worry. Has Mrs Franklin come back to stay, do you think?'

'I'm afraid not.'

'Your poor father. He must be quite beside himself, poor soul.' She clasped her hands. 'Men don't care to show their feelings, do they, and that makes it worse for them. When my brother died my father didn't shed a tear. He was like a rock and we all leaned on him. But the grief ate away at him, you see, because he couldn't express it. A few months later he went into a decline. Couldn't eat, hardly spoke, wouldn't go anywhere or see anyone. My poor mother was at her wits' end.'

Startled, Nancy looked into the dressmaker's face as she relived the tragedy.

'What happened to him?' she asked, dreading the answer.

'He died. Just withered away and died. It was terrible. Not something you can ever forget. How's your father taken it?'

'He's bearing up,' Nancy lied. 'I did offer to be with him through today's discussion but he preferred to be on his own. I'm hoping that the solicitor's presence will smooth the way for them. Now then, time for your cup of tea. Shall I ring for it?'

'Thank you, Miss Franklin. I wouldn't say no. I'm due at Mrs Bennett's in half an hour. I'm making a coat for her daughter. Navy blue with silk lapels. Off to London in a bit of a rush to marry her young soldier man. More than a bit of a rush, if you take my meaning. Still, that's the way young people are these days. The father doesn't care for him but what's to be done?'

So other families had their problems, Nancy thought wearily. Just then the new maid arrived. Dora was slim with short dark hair and brown eyes and her 'open-air complexion' emphasised what Nancy already knew about her – that she had previously worked on her parents' farm. She came in, glancing nervously around her, and Nancy smiled reassuringly.

'Are you finding your feet, Dora?' she asked. 'It does take time to get used to the routine but Cook will help you.'

'Yes, miss. I mean Miss Franklin.' She smoothed her apron.

91

'Good. A small pot of tea for Mrs Bailey, please, Dora.'

Dora was gazing admiringly at the cream satin which the dressmaker was lovingly folding into sheets of tissue paper.

'Your wedding dress, miss! Oh, it's going to be lovely!'

Mrs Bailey looked suitably modest and Nancy said, 'It is, isn't it? We're just talking about the bouquet. I think maybe a small posy would be best. We don't want to hide the dress.'

When she had gone Mrs Bailey said, 'I think that's a splendid idea. And what about freesias? They always look good against cream. The colours are so soft.'

Nancy promised to think about it and, when the tea arrived with a plate of biscuits, left Mrs Bailey to enjoy them alone while she hurried upstairs to see what was happening between her father and his wife. She would *not* interfere, she resolved firmly. It was between Lilian and her father. Nor would she speak a word to Lilian. A polite smile was all she would offer. Pausing outside the door she listened. The unfamiliar mumble was presumably the solicitor's voice. Tapping sharply on the door she went straight in, a fixed smile on her face.

'Good morning. I wondered whether you would like a tray of tea, Papa.'

Lilian said, 'This is Nancy, my stepdaughter.' To Nancy she said, 'Arthur Weddle, my solicitor.'

Nancy gave him a brief nod then looked at her father. He was sitting ramrod straight in his chair behind the desk, an expression of repressed anger on his face. His hands were two large fists on the desk top. Lilian and the solicitor sat in front of the desk but not too close. The atmosphere was tense and Nancy could imagine how much strain it was putting on her father. A quick glance in Lilian's direction showed her that her stepmother was also angry for there was a small red spot on each of her cheeks.

The solicitor looked distinctly uncomfortable and seized the opportunity to say, 'Tea! Now that would be very acceptable.'

Nancy glanced at her father for his answer.

He said, 'There won't be time, Nancy. They'll be leaving shortly.'

Lilian's small chin jutted stubbornly. 'Oh, I doubt that, James. There's still plenty to be discussed before we go.'

Her father said, 'Very well, then, but a tray for four, Nancy. I'd like you to join us. I think you should know just how your stepmother plans to disrupt Theo's life!'

There was an awkward silence as Nancy wondered what to say.

Lilian turned to the solicitor. 'You see what I have had to put up with all these years.'

In a low voice he said, 'I really don't advise you to take that tone, Mrs Franklin. We are here to make arrangements for the care of your son. At least, that is my understanding of the situation. We all have his best interests at heart.'

'And mine!' Lilian added.

He nodded. 'And yours.' He looked up. 'Mrs Franklin misses her son, as any mother would do.'

Nancy stared at Lilian in surprise.

Her father said, 'You should have thought have that before you left!'

Lilian swallowed, obviously ill at ease.

The solicitor said, 'Don't distress yourself, Mrs Franklin. We are here to try and put the matter right.'

Avoiding his wife's eyes, James said, 'There's only one way to be reunited with Theo, Lilian. Come home.'

Everyone was silent as the words sank in. So he would take her back, thought Nancy. She watched Lilian's expression, trying to read it.

The solicitor said, 'Is that a firm offer, Mr Franklin?'

'It is. I want her to come back to me. I'm willing to . . .

We can make a fresh start.' He was staring down at his clenched fists.

Lilian whispered, 'I can't do that, James. I'm sorry.'

With an oath James pushed back his chair and crossed to the window. He thrust his hands into his pockets, staring out at the trees.

Lilian watched him. 'I can't give him up, James. But Theo should be with me.'

Nancy looked at her. 'Are you sure that Cooper will make a good father?'

Mr Weddle coughed. 'I understand that he is very keen.'

Nancy said, 'I was asking Lilian.'

The silence lengthened. Lilian looked flustered. 'He isn't used to children. He's never been married. How does he know how he would feel?'

'In other words he's not keen.' Nancy was almost sorry for her.

James turned. 'You want to take him away from his home and his inheritance so that he can live with a man who doesn't want him around?'

'Papa's right. Theo—'

Lilian rounded on her. 'You keep out of this, Nancy. You'll be married shortly and then what? James will be down at the stables all day. Who will bring Theo up? He needs his mother and I need him.' Her voice shook.

'This concerns me,' Nancy replied hotly. 'Theo is my brother and I want him to be happy as much as my father does. I want him to stay at Franklins with us and we'll fight any suggestion that he lives with you and – and your lover!'

Lilian flinched at the word and the implied disrespect but before she could answer Nancy went on. 'We've already discussed this and I have decided to delay my wedding until we have found a suitable solution.' She hoped her father wasn't looking too surprised. 'We may employ another nanny. Or a tutor so Theo can be taught at home.'

Lilian was startled. 'Delay your wedding?'

'It may be best in the circumstances. I'm sure Lawrence would see the sense in that.' There was no need for Lilian to know that it was Lawrence himself who had suggested the postponement – which was becoming more likely with every passing day. Nancy refused to admit how adversely Lilian's behaviour had affected her relationship with her fiancé.

The solicitor was scribbling in his notebook and Lilian glanced at him uneasily.

'Donald and I are planning to move to the South of France,' she announced suddenly. 'The climate will be perfect for Theo with his weak chest.'

'Weak chest?' James frowned. 'First I've heard of it. His chest is as sound as a bell.'

'How would you know? You were never around. You neglected Theo and you neglected me.'

Nancy had heard enough. 'Who are you, Lilian, to talk about neglect? Where were you when Theo had his Sports Day? Gadding with Donald Cooper, I suppose. Oh yes! The headmaster told me you didn't turn up. You used Theo as an excuse to spend time with Cooper. The fact that poor Theo waited for you to arrive didn't bother you, did it?'

Her father cried, 'Is this true, Lilian?'

The solicitor said, 'I hope you can substantiate these allegations, Miss Franklin.'

But Lilian, it seemed, was growing weary of the struggle. 'I'm not staying here to be insulted by your chit of a daughter,' she told James, rising to her feet. Snatching up her handbag she turned on the solicitor who was frantically struggling to return his papers to his briefcase.

'In that case,' he stammered, 'I think we should call it a day. We'll be in touch . . . Thank you for your time.'

Nancy followed them down the stairs but Lilian, white-faced, pulled open the front door and hurried outside.

Nancy stood on the step and watched them drive away.

Lilian sat hunched on the seat, her head down, and Nancy was surprised to feel a growing compassion for the woman. She had risked everything in a gamble for love and now the expected happiness with Donald Cooper had not materialised. She had thrown away her reputation and was now surrounded by strangers in an unfamiliar town. She had Donald Cooper – but she was missing her son.

Six

The following day found Nancy holding the fort in the office, as her father had gone to Newmarket with Carroway, Liddy and Deakes, the jockey. They would meet Millicent Deepny and the prospective buyer. They would be away all day and Nancy was dreading any awkward telephone calls. She was finding it difficult to settle and wandered round the house, mulling over the events of the previous day. In particular she thought about the disastrous meeting with Lilian and her own intervention. Far from smoothing troubled waters she had probably made matters worse.

Also on her mind was the fact that so far Lawrence had failed to answer her letter. She wondered uncomfortably if he had shown it to his parents and whether they were all conferring behind her back. Sighing, she thought how impossibly her life had changed in less than a week. Problems with her father, with Theo and now with Lawrence and his family – and all because of Lilian. But there was never going to be a magic wand which would restore her life to normal. She simply had to get on with it and fight her way through the difficulties.

She called in to the kitchen to have a few words with Cook about Dora and was told she was 'a fast learner and very willing'. That was one problem less to fret about, Nancy told herself thankfully. She was on her way back to the office when the telephone rang and she answered it with a rapidly beating heart and crossed fingers. It was John Brayde.

'Any chance of a chat with Jack Liddy?' he asked. 'I've got Lucy with me and I thought we could both pop along to Franklins if it was convenient.' Nancy explained that Liddy and her father were at Newmarket but agreed that Brayde could come and see his horses anyway. The thought of a little moral support was pleasant and she wanted to meet Lucy. She had been planning to invite the girl round for a picnic when Theo returned from school. Although Lucy was a few years older, Nancy thought they would probably get along and it would be good for Theo to have some young female company for a change.

They arrived half an hour later and Nancy was secretly impressed with John Brayde's daughter. He had made a good job of bringing her up alone. Fair-haired and with a pale complexion and grey eyes, she had a round face which showed both sweetness and promise. She also had beautiful manners and a composure that was unusual in one so young.

They walked in the garden, admiring the rhododendrons, and Lucy chatted to Symes, who was weeding the rose bed. After looking in at the stables, Brayde joined them and, swearing him to secrecy, Nancy told him of the row with Lilian, grateful to talk about it to someone sympathetic. It was a huge relief to share her troubles – she had tried unsuccessfully to talk to her father and hadn't wanted to burden Moira Callender.

He frowned. 'Do you believe your stepmother – about moving abroad? It might be a threat or even a bargaining tool. Agreeing *not* to take Theo abroad in return for some kind of favourable settlement.'

Nancy frowned. 'Would she be capable of that, I wonder?' Idly she picked up a twig and sent it spinning. 'She was in a strange mood. At times on the offensive and then suddenly strangely vulnerable. She said she was missing Theo and I believed her. But I suppose she might do anything if Cooper put her up to it.'

'Did you want her to accept your father's offer?'

'That's a good question, Mr Brayde. Deep down I think I did!'

Lucy meanwhile had run on ahead towards the stables and Nancy followed with Brayde. It was quiet in the yard. The horses dozed or shuffled their feet, a few flies buzzed in the sunshine and a black cat sprang up from inside one of the stalls and fled at the sight of the humans.

Brayde laughed. 'Do you have that effect on all your pets?'

Nancy laughed. 'It's a stray,' she protested. 'We don't have pets.'

'A pity, then. Black cats are supposed to be lucky, aren't they?'

Nancy rolled her eyes. 'I'll adopt it immediately!'

They made the rounds, patting and fondling those horses that were awake and interested.

Lucy asked if she could explore the large barn.

Nancy nodded. 'But it's very dusty from the straw bales. Don't spoil your dress. You can go into the orchard, too, if you wish. You won't find any fruit this early but it's very peaceful.'

They watched her hurry away and Brayde said, 'Oh, to be young again!'

'And carefree. Right now I can't imagine ever feeling carefree again!'

'Maybe you should ride again,' Brayde suggested. 'The exercise is very relaxing and it blows away the cobwebs. Lucy loves to ride but when I'm tied up with business she has to go out alone. She has her own pony but we also have a wonderfully docile mare called Bonny. If you want a gentle mount while you ease yourself back into the saddle you'd be welcome to ride her.'

To Nancy's surprise the idea didn't shock her as it once might have done. She promised to remember his offer then changed the subject. They walked slowly back to the house in search of home-made lemon barley water and on the way found Lucy in the barn, her eyes shining with excitement.

'This is perfect!' she told them. 'We could have a party to celebrate something or other. The harvest, maybe, or better still—' She glanced impishly at her father.

'Lucy Brayde! You shameless hussy!' Laughing, he reached out for her, but she dodged away. 'Whatever have I done to deserve such a daughter?'

Mystified, Nancy watched as he gave her shoulder an affectionate squeeze. She echoed Lucy's words, 'Better still?' and waited for an explanation.

'My forward daughter has a birthday coming up next month and she has always wanted a party in a barn. We have several but each one is too small.'

Lucy said, 'But this one is perfect – plenty of room and all those wonderful bales of straw. We could cover them for seats and hang Chinese lanterns overhead so that when it grows dark—'

Her enthusiasm was infectious and Nancy nodded. 'I don't see why not,' she said. 'Cook would be very willing to—'

'Oh no!' cried Lucy. 'We wouldn't put you to any trouble, I promise. I'd organise it – with Theo's help – and our housekeeper could make some cakes and things. And we could play marvellous games and dance. Tim can play the concertina.'

Brayde said, 'Tim's our gardener's eldest son. Lucy finds him rather charming!'

'Papa! I do not!' Lucy protested. 'He's a dreadful boy but

he *can* play the concertina. He must be invited otherwise we shall have no music.'

Nancy smiled. 'I love the idea. It would be something cheerful to look forward to. The barn was one of my mother's favourite places. She painted several pictures of it over the years.'

'We have one of them,' Brayde told her. 'My father bought it from her a few months before you were born. He always maintained that she could have made a name for herself as an artist. What did he say exactly? A great eye for the beauty of everyday things. He was truly impressed.'

Surprised and delighted, Nancy said eagerly, 'I'd love to see it one day. I don't seem to have inherited her talent. I gave up painting lessons when I was eleven. The tutor said I showed little promise so Papa decided I should have singing lessons instead. I can sing but my repertoire's quite small. I don't enjoy it particularly.' She smiled. 'The truth is I don't really shine at anything.'

'I wouldn't say that,' Brayde protested. 'You have a personality many would envy and, dare I say it, great charm.'

'You hardly know me!' she protested, delighted by his words. 'Thank you kindly.'

They settled themselves under the large chestnut tree and Cook appeared with the drinks and a message. She looked hot and flustered as she picked her way heavily across the grass with a laden tray.

'Mr Wilton rang but will try again later,' she told Nancy.

Nancy looked at her guiltily. 'Did any of the owners ring?'

'No, they didn't. Just as well, eh?' She gave Lucy a wide smile and dabbed her face with her handkerchief.

Nancy said, 'It's so warm today, Cook. You should have sent Dora out with the drinks. That's what she's here for.'

'I've sent her home, Miss Franklin. I hope you didn't mind.' She leaned forward and whispered, 'It's her month-lies and she had bad cramps. Pale as a ghost, she was. I felt sorry for the girl.'

Nancy glanced at Brayde who was politely staring at the far end of the lawn, apparently paying them no attention. 'You did the right thing, Cook.'

For a while, after she had gone, they drank in silence and then Lucy left them and went in search of the orchard.

Brayde said, 'I was wondering whether to run Gordie Brae in one of the French classics. Theoretically he should do quite well against the opposition but the travelling doesn't suit him. Last year he was upset by the sea crossing and wasn't even placed. It would mean taking him the day before and stabling him overnight to give him time to collect himself.'

'Remind Papa. He hasn't mentioned it to me but that doesn't mean he isn't thinking about— Oh!' She drew back suddenly as Brayde reached out towards her. 'What on earth—?'

She felt his hand brush against the skin of her neck inside the collar of her blouse. There was an angry buzz as something flew away.

'A wasp,' he explained. 'Just about to crawl inside your collar. I'm sorry if I startled you.'

As Nancy thanked him she caught sight of Lawrence walking towards them across the lawn.

'It seems I've arrived just in time!' He glared at John Brayde.

Nancy stared at him. 'What does that mean?'

'I find Brayde with an arm around your shoulder. That's what I mean.'

'Lawrence! There was a wasp crawling inside my collar.'

'Can't he speak for himself?'

102

Red-faced, Lawrence stood beside the table and slowly Brayde stood up.

'I don't have to explain myself to you, Wilton. Miss Franklin has told you what was happening. Would you prefer it if your fiancée had been stung?'

Nancy's heart thumped as the two men faced each other angrily.

Lawrence said, 'Well, it looked mighty cosy to me. The two of you sitting here alone together.'

'Mr Brayde's daughter is with us,' Nancy told him. 'At least, she was. She's wandered off into the orchard.'

'How convenient!'

His tone had changed slightly and Nancy knew he had accepted the truth of the situation but did not know how to extricate himself.

He turned to her. 'I was expecting you to return my call.'

'Cook said you were going to ring back later.'

Brayde said, 'Perhaps Lucy and I should be going. You two obviously need to talk. Excuse me, Miss Franklin.'

Lawrence said, 'Don't put yourself out on my account. I haven't come to stay.' He turned towards Nancy. 'Mother has invited you and your father for lunch on Sunday – to talk things over.' He glanced at Brayde who had wandered off in the direction of the orchard and was calling his daughter. He lowered his voice. 'And I don't want that fellow hanging round here.'

'You have no right to dictate who can and can't visit Franklins,' Nancy told him. 'John Brayde is one of Papa's best owners and he is always welcome.'

'I suppose he came to see your father.'

'He did.'

'Then why is he with you?'

'Because my father's not here. Mr Brayde brought his daughter at my request. She wants to hold her birthday party in our big barn. I have offered them some refreshments, that is all.'

'You seem mighty fond of the man.'

Nancy wanted to slap him. 'That's very unworthy of you, Lawrence, and I think you know it. Perhaps you should discuss the matter with Papa. He might agree to ban the man from our stables just to please you but I doubt it very much.'

From the corner of her eye she saw Brayde and his daughter returning. 'Are we still invited to Sunday lunch with your parents or would you prefer to cancel it?'

His eyes were suddenly full of remorse and Nancy felt her anger begin to fade. At least he still loved her enough to feel jealous, she told herself.

'Yes, do come,' he said. 'They are adamant that we postpone the wedding but we can talk it over.' He pulled her suddenly into his arms and kissed her.

It was a long kiss and when Nancy tried to withdraw he tightened his hold on her. Lawrence kept her in his arms until Brayde and Lucy had time to see them then released her. With a curt nod in their direction he strode away without another word. Embarrassed, Nancy tried to compose herself.

'We have to go also,' Brayde told her, 'but thank you for treating us so kindly. I'll speak with your father tomorrow. I hope I haven't given you further problems.' He glanced at Lawrence's retreating figure.

'Nothing that won't mend,' she told him. To Lucy she said, 'I'll write to Theo about the party. He'll be so excited.'

Lucy smiled. 'Tell him I'll need some help and I'll be relying on him!'

When they had gone Nancy returned to the kitchen and asked Cook to make her a sandwich instead of a proper lunch.

'I'll eat it in the office.'

'Lost your appetite, have you?' Cook asked.

Nancy could only nod.

An hour later, when the telephone did ring, the call was not from one of the owners but from Hartleigh School.

'Miss Franklin, this is Ronald Grey, your son's headmaster. I think I should speak to your father about Theo. We've had a call from his mother.'

'My father hasn't returned from Newmarket yet and may be quite late. Maybe I can help.'

After a pause, Grey said, 'I had a conversation with Mrs Franklin earlier this morning – a rather distressing conversation – but have only just found time to contact you.'

'Distressing?'

'I don't think I should go into details but Mrs Franklin was very upset. In tears, in fact.'

Nancy digested this information with a sense of shock. She had never seen Lilian cry. She glanced at the clock. 'You say it was this morning? But it's now gone six. Why did you wait so long to—'

'We've had problems of our own,' he informed her crisply. 'One of our senior boys was attacked by a bullock on a cross-country run. He was taking a short cut and shouldn't have been in the field at all but that doesn't lessen the serious nature of his injuries.'

'I'm so sorry.' Nancy cursed her hasty tongue. She had blamed Lawrence for jumping to conclusions and here she was making the same mistake. 'Of course you have other boys in your care. Please forgive me, Mr Grey. Poor lad. Will he recover?' She thought with a shudder about the horrors of her own accident and the months of painful rehabilitation.

'He's got a broken leg and suspected internal injuries but the doctor is cautiously hopeful, whatever that means. His parents are in India but his grandparents are coming down

105

from Scotland. The boy will stay in our sanatorium until he can be moved. But that's by the by. We need to talk about Theo. As you know, Mrs Franklin intends to collect Theo from school next Monday. Naturally at such short notice the school fees will—'

Nancy gasped. 'Collect him from school? But why? What reason did she give? We know nothing about this.'

'Do you not?' He sounded wary. 'I was given the distinct impression that it had been agreed. I admit I was somewhat taken aback that I had heard nothing from your father but I had no reason to doubt her.'

'Mrs Franklin has no right to take him out of school, Mr Grey.' Nancy put a hand to her head, wondering once again how much she should tell him. 'Mr Grey, the situation here is extremely difficult. I wish I could say I'm cautiously hopeful but I can't. Mrs Franklin has left my father. She wants to take Theo away with her. Naturally my father refuses even to consider the idea. Did she say where they were going?'

There was a short silence.

'I'm trying to recall the conversation but I don't believe she told me her plans for him. Oh dear. It was rather remiss of me, I suppose, but I had just finished school assembly and was on my way to the second-year boys for their scripture lesson. And you had no idea?' He tutted. 'Then I've given you a bit of a shock, I'm afraid. Thank heavens I rang you. I think your father will have to discuss the situation with her. If she turns up at Hartleigh I shan't know what to say – or do. This is very awkward for me.'

'It's not easy for us, Mr Grey. Quite unexpected.' Nancy's mind was busy with possibilities. 'I expect we shall have to consult a solicitor. Legally I feel his future should be decided by my father but I'm really not at all sure.'

'There is one other thing I think you should know, Miss Franklin.'

Nancy closed her eyes.

'Theo *has* heard the rumour that his mother is no longer at Franklins. Another boy told him. I'm afraid there has been gossip among some of the parents and it has filtered down to the boys. Theo was sensible enough to go to Matron and—'

'When was this?'

'Last evening. She—'

'What did Matron tell him?' Nancy's voice was rising and she told herself to stay calm. Panicking would help no one.

'She told him she knew nothing, but said she would find out and tell him today. This morning, of course, his mother telephoned and then we were overtaken by a new disaster.'

Nancy breathed deeply before replying. 'I'll ask my father to telephone you as soon as he arrives home. He'll be shocked by what's happening and I can assure you that you should resist any attempt by Mrs Franklin to take Theo away from Hartleigh.'

'I would like to add something else, Miss Franklin, which I'm sure you will understand. That is that I must put the reputation of the school above all – except for the well-being of the pupils, of course – and I do hope none of this reaches the newspapers. It would be highly damaging to have Hartleigh involved in such a disasteful scandal. If you are approached I would be grateful if you could try not to mention the school although I accept that you cannot actually lie or be seen to be dissembling.'

During this last speech Nancy's hand had tightened round the receiver until her fingers were white. With an effort she bit back angry words and struggled to throw off a feeling of shame. The Franklin family were now being viewed as an embarrassment and they had Lilian to thank for that.

She said, 'We'll bear that in mind, Mr Grey,' and hung up before he could speak again.

107

Staring bleakly at the telephone she wondered briefly how people had managed in emergencies before it was invented. She desperately needed to unburden herself and Nanny came to mind but after a moment's consideration she rejected the idea as selfish. There was no point in worrying an elderly lady when she could be of no help. There was nothing for it but to talk to her father when he returned.

It was nearly nine o'clock when she finally saw the telltale lights in the stableyard and knew that her father was back. She decided to wait. It was always a scramble to unload the horsebox and bed the animal down for the night and a spare woman would get in the way. It was to be hoped Carroway had done well for that would have put her father in a good mood.

But then I'll have to spoil it for him, she mused. Damn Lilian! Why did she have to choose Papa – and why on earth did he fall for her charms?

Curled up in the office chair, her mind produced further questions. Why had she, Nancy, fallen for Lawrence and he for her? Would they ever end up like her father and Lilian? Was there a recipe for happy married life or was it all a lottery?

Footsteps at the back door interrupted her thoughts and, straightening herself, she called, 'Papa! How did it go?'

It was Jack Liddy who entered and one look at his ruddy face told her the news was bad. His face was set in grim lines and she could see the tension in his shoulders.

'Sorry we're late, Miss Franklin. It's been a sod of a day, if you'll pardon my French.' He wiped a hand across his face.

Trying to look on the bright side, she asked, 'Wasn't he even placed?'

Liddy removed his cap and shook his head. 'Carroway won,' he told her. 'Ran a spanking race!'

'Carroway *won*? Then what's the matter?'

'When he pulled up he was bleeding from the nose. Not a lot but I was shocked.'

'Oh *no*! Poor Carroway.'

It did happen occasionally, she knew. After great exertion a blood vessel might burst in the nose but with rest a horse could recover.

'But did he look well before the race?'

Liddy hesitated. 'We thought – that is, me and the guvnor – that he looked a bit dull. Not his usual perky self, as you might say. The guvnor asked Her Ladyship what she wanted to do. We didn't want him to run a poor race because of this buyer but Her Ladyship wasn't prepared to scratch him. She reckoned he was probably just tired from the journey. So we let him run and he went like a ruddy rocket.'

Nancy smiled. 'Papa always said he was a fighter.'

Liddy went on, 'We cleaned up his nose and walked him slowly to the winners' enclosure and he seemed fine. A bit dreamy, perhaps. You know, not so sharp as usual but not wobbly or anything. I've seen worse. Lady Deepny got her prize and I was beginning to feel a bit better about him. We got him into the horsebox to bring him him home and then suddenly down he went. No warning at all. Crash! Down on his side. Poor old boy just lay there, breathing heavily and rolling his eyes.'

The image this conjured up brought tears to Nancy's eyes but she blinked them away. Liddy handed her a couple of forms which she knew would include the Newmarket vet's report and the on-site enquiry.

'Is he . . . ?' Nancy couldn't say it.

'Dead? No, miss. But they said he should be put down.'

Briefly Nancy's mind refused to function. All she could think of was Carroway, with his beautiful inquisitive nature and his lively temperament. The thought of him lying sick in the horsebox appalled her.

'Is he in pain, Liddy?'

'I doubt it. I reckon the poor old feller's out of it.'

'Unconscious?'

He nodded. 'Lady Deepny refused to have him put out of his misery. She's a stupid old bat, that one! She's waiting with the guvnor for David Evans. She thinks he'll pull Carroway round but there's no chance. You'd best file those forms.'

'How's my father taking it?' Nancy asked. 'No. Sorry. Silly question. I can guess. And he won't want Lady Deepny around – but what can he do? She owns the horse. Is she very upset?'

'Crying and carrying on!' He shrugged. 'He asked her to let me take her home but she wouldn't budge. Not her . . . Won't help matters if this gets out on top of – well, the guvnor's missus going off like she has. You know what it's like in this game. Like a ruddy bush fire. "Franklins are having a bad run," they'll say and we'll get the thumbs down.'

Nancy didn't need to be told. A bush fire summed up perfectly the way bad news travelled among the racing fraternity.

'Does it have to get out?' she asked. 'We can trust the vet to keep quiet about it and surely Lady Deepny can be relied upon to be discreet. After all, it was her decision to run him.'

'What about the buyer? He'll have to know.'

'There must be something we can do,' she cried desperately.

'You tell me!' he answered and his sigh was heartfelt.

Liddy left her to her thoughts, which were deeply depressing. Her father would be devastated to lose one of his most promising horses and he would be furious with Millicent Deepny for prolonging the poor animal's misery. He would

110

also blame himself for not insisting that Carroway was withdrawn from the race. And the horse would die. Jack Liddy thought there was no hope and he should know. Her father would trust his judgement, especially when it matched his own. Part of her wanted to take a last look at Carroway but another part wanted to remember him as she had last seen him – alive and happy.

As for the call from the school, she was trying to decide whether to tell her father or not. If she didn't tell him tonight there would be trouble in the morning when she *did*. He would insist, reasonably enough, that Theo was the the most important factor in his life and she had no right to withhold such important information.

I'll tell him, she decided.

In the meantime she found herself reaching for a shawl. Without having made up her mind about Carroway, she had come to a decision.

In the stableyard the lanterns cast an eerie glow, lighting the faces of the three figures huddled together to the rear of the horsebox. The interior of the box was in shadow but Nancy could just make out the dark shape of the prostrate horse. Holding back her emotions she walked first to her father and slid a comforting arm around his waist.

'Nancy!' He sighed heavily. His face was drawn into harsh lines and in his eyes she read defeat.

The vet said, 'This is a bad business, but there's nothing for it.' He glanced at Millicent Deepny, whose face was ravaged by tears. 'You've got to let him go, ma'am. For his sake. He's never going to get up again. Do the right thing.'

'Oh, don't keep saying that!' she cried. 'All I ask is that you give him a few hours. He might surprise us all.'

'He won't. I can tell you that for nothing.'

111

She turned to Nancy. 'He might, mightn't he?' Her voice quivered.

Nancy moved to stand beside her and took hold of her hand. 'Trust them,' she pleaded. 'It would be a mercy to let him go. He's had a wonderful life. Luxury, loving kindness, the best of everything. We'll all miss him but I'd hate to see him suffer. Do him one last kindness.'

Millicent Deepny turned and laid her head on Nancy's shoulder. 'Do it then,' she whispered and Nancy nodded to her father. Her father ran back to the house and they all waited without speaking for his return. When he reappeared he was carrying a revolver and he at once climbed into the horsebox. Nancy closed her eyes. Millicent Deepny covered her ears with her hands. The shot itself was unexciting but the moments that followed were fraught for all of them.

As James stepped down it was the vet's turn to enter the horsebox. After a moment or two he climbed down again.

'All over.'

Nancy led Millicent Deepny back to the house and into the office and poured her a generous whisky. She tossed it down and then shuddered.

'I suppose we must be thankful this has happened now,' she said, 'and not after Mr Travers had bought him. That would have looked really bad. As it is he won't be too happy when I tell him what's happened. He went home knowing only that Carroway had won.'

Later the vet gave her a lift home while Jack Liddy and James did what needed to be done in the stables. The disposal of the body would wait until morning.

When Nancy's father came back into the office and had been similarly installed with a drink, he asked, 'Any messages?' He drained the glass and poured himself another. He glanced at her. 'Nothing?'

Nancy opened her mouth then closed it and in those few

seconds she changed her mind. She would say nothing about Theo until the morning.

But her silence had alerted him. 'Something's up, Nancy. What is it?' he demanded and his fingers tightened on the glass tumbler. 'Tell me, Nancy, for God's sake!'

As gently as she could Nancy explained what had happened and to her relief her father listened impassively. She waited for him to explode but instead he stared wordlessly over her head. Then, without warning, he sprang to his feet with a low groan and hurled the whisky tumbler. It flew past Nancy's head, narrowly missing her, and smashed against the wall. Nancy stared at the fragments of glass, her body trembling with shock.

'Papa!' she cried. 'Please! Sit down. We can sort it out!'

He looked at her wildly, his eyes wide, his face contorted with rage. Or was it fear – the fear of losing all that one loved and valued? He groaned again and whispered something she couldn't catch. She had no way of knowing what he had said but she *could* recognise his state of mind and the extent of his desperation. Terrified, she put out a hand to him, but he pushed past her, stumbled to the door, pulled it open and ran out into the night.

Nancy ran to the door. 'Papa! Don't go! Papa, *please!*'

'Leave me alone, for God's sake!' he shouted.

Fearfully Nancy watched his figure dwindle as he stumbled into the shadows and was lost from sight. No doubt he needed to be on his own, she told herself, resisting the urge to follow him but already longing for his return. She waited in the doorway but time passed and there was no sign of him. As she stared out into the darkness the events of the day finally took their toll on mind and body and she was overcome with a paralysing weariness. With an effort she dragged herself upstairs to her bedroom, threw herself on to the bed and, with passionate tears, gave herself up to a growing despair.

At five to eight the next morning Ronald Grey held out his hand to his visitor.

'Please sit down, Sergeant.'

Sergeant Swale eased his bulk cautiously on to the chair indicated and took out his notebook. 'I understand you have lost one of your pupils, Mr Grey.'

The headmaster frowned. 'I wouldn't put it quite like that but one of our boys *is* missing. A nine-year-old by the name of Franklin. Theodore Franklin. He was last seen—'

Sergeant Swale glanced up. 'Not the trainer's son? Not *that* Franklin?'

'I'm afraid so. I—'

The sergeant grinned. 'I have a little flutter on his horses from time to time. My sister's boy's one of their stable lads. I sometimes win a few bob.' Catching a warning look in the headmaster's eye, he coughed. 'Now then, about this lad of theirs.'

The headmaster steepled his fingers. 'The fact is I don't want this to get out, if you see what I mean, because I don't want to alarm his parents. Not just yet. So I'm hoping your men can find him quickly. He can't be far away. Matron discovered that he was missing when the boys rose this morning at seven. He wasn't in the washroom and the other boys hadn't seen him. It looks as though he ran off during the night.'

'In the dark? Plucky little kid, then. I don't think I'd have run off into the dark when I was nine.' He wrote, turned the page and wrote again. 'Description?'

'Oh . . . Not very tall . . .'

'He wouldn't be, at nine, sir. Can't you be a bit more precise? Hair colour. Eyes. Fat. Thin. What would he be wearing?'

114

Matron had to be called in to supply these details and they were duly noted.

'Thank you, madam.' Sergeant Swale watched her leave then turned his attention once more to the headmaster. 'And you're certain he ran away, are you? No chance that he was kidnapped?'

Grey paled. 'Kidnapped? *Kidnapped?* Good Lord, I should hope not! Of course he wasn't . . . That is, it's most unlikely. Unless—' He leaned forward and rested his face in his hands.

The sergeant said, 'You don't mean it's possible, do you, sir? If you think that way you should notify the parents at once. They have a right—'

'No, no, no!' Grey sat up again, visibly shaken. 'What am I thinking of? Of course he wasn't kidnapped. It's more likely he ran away. There has been some trouble in the family which has upset him. His parents have separated and the poor lad is being pulled two ways. Both parents want him, if you see what I mean. I really can't say more – it's a private matter for the family – but if you could set up a search party I'm sure he'll turn up safe and well.'

'I certainly hope so, sir. He might have got on the bus or be waiting for a train. D'you know if he had any money? Or has any gone missing?'

'Not to my knowledge. But I'll send for Tompson. He's the senior boy in Franklin's dormitory.'

When Tompson arrived he brought disconcerting news. Theo had sold the contents of his tuck box, an almost new Teddy Bears annual and a set of tin soldiers.

'Sold them?' The sergeant stared at him.

'Yes, sir. We are allowed to swap our things.'

The headmaster snapped, 'Swap, yes, but not *sell!*'

Unperturbed, Tompson said, 'He swapped them for money, sir.'

115

Grey waved him away and drew a long breath. 'So he had some money.'

'As I said, sir. A plucky little kid.' He stood up. 'We'll do our best to find him but in the meantime I should let his parents know what's happened.' The notebook went back into his pocket and he reached for his helmet. 'I can find my own way out, Mr Grey. We'll keep you informed and hope he hasn't got too far.'

Ronald Grey watched him cycle away. He was beginning to wish the Franklins had chosen another school for their 'plucky little lad'.

Seven

The first thing Nancy heard when she woke was the rain beating on the window. She eyed it blearily, aware of what it was doing to the various racetracks in the area. It would make heavy going and anxious trainers and owners would be 'walking the courses'. They would have to decide whether or not the wet conditions would suit their horses and whether the track was safe for them to run. Sliding from the bed, Nancy realised that the rain would make the job of burying Carroway that much harder and certainly more dismal.

In the hallway, Nancy met Dora and took the breakfast tray from her.

'I'm going up to see Nanny so I'll save your legs,' she told the girl. 'You can bring it down later when Nanny rings.'

Dora said, 'I'm so sorry about the horse. Cook told me.'

'We're all very upset but these things happen. Cook seems to be very pleased with your progress. I hope you'll be staying on with us.'

'Oh, thank you, Miss Franklin.'

Nancy nodded and the girl's beaming smile stayed with her as she went up the stairs. It was good to have anything to be cheerful about, she reflected, but then matters couldn't get much worse. Once they had dealt with Lilian, life should get back to something near normal.

Nancy told Nanny about Carroway and the old lady

sighed. 'Children. Horses. They break your heart,' she said. 'How's your father taking it?'

'I haven't seen him this morning but I'm sure it was a great blow for him in more ways than one. Liddy will have broken it to the lads by now so there'll be deep gloom. I can hardly bear to go down there. I expect they're burying Carroway as Lady Deepny requested.'

'I know, dear. Poor Lady Deepny. I remember her as a rather difficult soul but she always spoke so lovingly about her horses.' Nanny's eyes narrowed as she regarded Nancy over the top of her boiled egg. 'And how's Lawrence?'

'He's fine,' Nancy said brightly. 'Father and I are going to the Wiltons for lunch on Sunday.'

'That's good news, then.' She dipped a finger of toast into her egg. 'I expect Theo's got his letter by now. You did send it, didn't you?'

'Yes, I did. And I wrote to him the following day. I shall tell him Carroway won his race but I think I'll save the news of his collapse until he comes home.'

She made her way downstairs to find Cook and Annie Symes waiting for her in the hallway. The latter's shoes were muddy, there were raindrops in her hair and her flimsy shawl gave little protection.

Cook eyed Nancy nervously. 'Mrs Symes begged to be allowed in. She wants a word, Miss Franklin. I said I didn't know if you—'

'That's all right, Cook.' Nancy looked at Annie Symes. It was already obvious that she was expecting another child. 'Come in here,' she told her, opening the door to the drawing room. She indicated a chair and they both sat.

Annie said, 'It's about George and him not coming in today because of his stomach. I've sent young Jeannie for the doctor, he's that bad, but you know what men are, miss. They won't admit to nothing, and he's been having these terrible turns – pains and that. Like a ghost he is when the pains come, and his inside's like water if you'll pardon the expression. And once or twice there's been blood and that—'

'Yes, yes!' Nancy said hastily. 'I can see the problem, Mrs Symes.' Her imagination was already working overtime. 'I'm sure you did right to send for the doctor. I'm sure we can manage without your husband for a day or two. Do let me know how he gets on.'

Annie Symes hesitated, turned to go then turned back. 'I've been meaning to ask you – that is, wondering if you, I mean your pa, would give him a second chance. He won't ask himself. Too proud by far. He has been trying to find other work but . . . Well, it's not easy.'

Nancy hesitated. George Symes had betrayed his master and had taken money for his treachery. She said, 'I think you will have to speak to my father, Mrs Symes, and I don't think this is a good time. Did you know we lost a horse yesterday on top of everything else? Poor Carroway—' Even as she uttered the words she saw, with a flash of insight, how pathetic they would sound to Annie Symes. To her a horse was a rich man's plaything and its death would mean nothing at all compared with her own problems.

Annie drew the ends of the shawl together, pressing her small fist against her chest. 'But with the baby coming and all, we won't have a roof over our heads.'

Nancy stared at her. She felt as though she were drowning in a sea of disasters but she could also see that the Symes family were facing a crisis. She told herself that George Symes had only himself to blame but she knew that was of little consolation to a woman about to bring another child into the world. For a moment the two women stared helplessly at each other. Suppose Symes was seriously ill? Nancy thought. What would happen if he died?

119

'I'll pass on your message if you like,' she said reluctantly, 'but when your husband recovers he must speak personally to my father. It's between the two of them.'

'If she comes back – Mrs Franklin, I mean – would that make it all right?'

Nancy shook her head. 'I don't know. I honestly don't know any more. I wish I could make it all go away but I can't. This awful mess . . .' She shrugged.

Annie Symes's face was reflecting her own anguish and suddenly Nancy could no longer bear it. 'You'd better go home,' she said gently. 'The doctor might be there by now.'

She swallowed hard as she watched the woman's retreat to the kitchen.

'God help us all!' she muttered and decided to find her father.

Dressed for rain, she was halfway to the stables when she heard footsteps behind her and found Dora running towards her across the wet grass, her face wreathed in smiles beneath the newspaper she held over her head.

'It's Mr Wilton, miss.'

'Oh!' Surprised, Nancy didn't know whether to be pleased or sorry. Perhaps he had come to cancel Sunday lunch . . . but no. A telephone call would suffice if that were the case.

'You run back before you get soaked,' she told Dora. 'Show him into the drawing room and say I'll be along shortly.'

'Yes, miss. He's ever so nice, miss.'

Nancy smiled. 'I'm glad you approve.'

Dora ran back to the house and Nancy followed more slowly, trying to decide how she would greet him.

He was standing by the window and turned as she entered, holding out his arms. She allowed herself to be hugged, trying to convince herself that all was well between them.

120

'I'm sorry,' he said. 'I behaved badly yesterday. Do say you forgive me, dearest.'

'I do, Lawrence. I shouldn't have spoken the way I did.' She led him to the sofa and they sat together. 'I hardly know any more what I say or do. I'm finding everything such a terrible strain.'

'I understand and I think you're wonderful. In your shoes I think I would have despaired but you carry on.'

'Lawrence, I *do* despair!' she told him. 'You have no idea how depressed I am, but my father has worse problems and I have to be strong for his sake.'

'I've come with more bad news, Nancy, and a confession. I don't know how you will take this but . . .' He sighed deeply. 'Donald tells me that Lilian plans to take Theo.'

'Lawrence, I already know—'

'No, please let me finish. Donald told me in strictest confidence and that put me in a spot. I couldn't tell you. You do see, don't you? Lilian wants him to *live* with them and she's talking about a new school for him in Dorset.'

'What exactly are you saying?' She stared at him. 'When did you know all this, Lawrence?'

'It doesn't matter when. What matters is I'm telling you now.'

'It matters to me.' Her heart was thumping uncomfortably. 'Tell me when you knew that they were planning to take Theo away from us!'

He lowered his eyes. 'I knew two days ago. I'm sorry, darling—'

'Two days ago?' And he had said nothing. Shocked, Nancy sank back against the cushions. 'I can't believe this, Lawrence. You would have allowed Lilian to take Theo—'

'Please, Nancy!' He rushed on. 'I've wanted to tell you everything, right from the start, but how could I? It's hardly chivalrous to betray a confidence from a friend. All I can say in my defence is that I did try to persuade him not to go through with it. I said, "Look, Donald, don't let her fool you the way she fooled Franklin. You should steer clear of women like that. You can do better for yourself."'

Nancy swallowed her growing anger. 'You knew they were going to take Theo and you didn't warn us.'

'Darling, you must understand.' Lawrence sat forward. 'Donald is one of my closet friends. We were at school together. We played cricket together.'

'Cricket! Oh, well! That makes it all right!' Nancy clenched her hands as her anger grew. He was beginning to sound like an adolescent schoolboy. 'Theo might be snatched from his school and removed from his family but you mustn't warn me in case you upset Donald Cooper!' Her voice rose. 'Never mind if Theo is unhappy or frightened. Never mind if the woman you're supposed to love is hurt in the process. Or your future father-in-law is devastated by the loss of his only son. Donald Cooper played cricket with you so that makes it acceptable!' Her voice was rising dangerously. 'If you don't mind me saying so, you, Lawrence, have some very warped ideas!'

His expression changed as he straightened up. 'I most certainly do mind. No one has ever accused me of not behaving like a perfect gentleman and I resent your—'

Nancy's heart was racing. 'Your priorities are interesting. First worry about your precious Donald. Second, worry about us. Isn't that how it was?'

Afraid of her mounting anger, she jumped to her feet, crossed the room and began to rearrange a bowl of flowers. One thought dominated her mind. Lawrence had betrayed them. For weeks he had pretended all was well and had allowed them to be ambushed by Lilian's defection. He had known the devastating truth all along and had said nothing. And now he would have sacrificed Theo.

'Nancy! My dearest girl . . . You mustn't take it like this. I've been honest.'

She lifted her head. 'Today, maybe – but what about all the lies by omission? You went to Dorset to "help a friend settle in his new house" without telling me that he would be sharing it with Lilian. You've talked with my father knowing that he was about to be publicly humiliated by your precious Donald. I might have forgiven you all that. But Theo . . . If you had the faintest idea of what you have done to us – to this family—' Her voice broke. 'How can I ever trust you after this?'

The distance between them seemed vast as they stared at each other.

Lawrence was looking at her coldly. 'I would have thought this disaster was all down to Lilian, not to me. If your stepmother had loved your father enough she would never have allowed Donald to seduce her.'

'Ah!' She seized on his careless words. 'So *he* seduced *her*! I thought Lilian was the wicked one and Donald the poor fool who was led astray!'

'Nancy, stop this.' His face was haggard. 'I don't want us to quarrel.'

'You should have thought of that earlier!'

'You're being utterly unreasonable. I can't talk to you when you're in this mood. I'm leaving now. Think hard, Nancy. When you've calmed down we can—'

'Just go, Lawrence. I've heard enough from you. And I will think hard, believe me. Long and hard.' Her hand moved towards the bell-pull but she changed her mind, walked to the front door and opened it. Lawrence hesitated as he reached her but, in case he intended a conciliatory kiss, she averted her face.

She closed the door behind him before he had reached the pony-trap. She walked back into the drawing room and waited until the sound of the horse's hooves and the rattle

123

of wheels had faded. Then, with a struggle, she removed her engagement ring and regarded it soberly. She would send it back to Lawrence. There was no way now that their relationship was going to survive the coming weeks.

It was after twelve when she realised that she hadn't seen her father all morning. It wasn't unusual but in view of Lilian's plan to collect Theo and Carroway's unexpected death, the niggling suspicion arose that her father might well have drunk too much the previous night. In which case, he might have failed to get up in time for morning exercise and might still be under the influence. She reproached herself for not thinking about him before.

'Papa!' she whispered and was immediately worried. It was quicker to check his bedroom than to visit the stables, especially as it was raining. She hurried up the stairs and tapped on his bedroom door. When there was no answer she opened it and reassured herself that his bed was empty. He wasn't in the library, the study or the office and she let out a sigh of relief. He was at the stables and she would see him at lunch. Satisfied, she closed the door and went downstairs. She must talk to him about Theo and decide what to do.

The bell rang as she reached the hall and she called out, 'I'll get it, Cook!'

A policeman stood on the step, water dripping from his cape, his bicycle propped up nearby.

He said, 'Mr Franklin at home? I need to have a word.'

'What about?'

'About his son.'

'Theo?' She caught her breath. 'Is he all right?'

'I have to speak with the father.'

'I don't know exactly where he is. I'm Theo's half-sister. Won't I do?'

He considered his options then nodded. 'I suppose so.'

'Then step inside from the rain for a moment.'

They both stepped into the hall and she closed the door.

Clearing his throat, he opened his notebook and began to read. 'The police have been in touch with us concerning your brother – that is, half-brother. The head of Hartleigh School says he has run away.'

Nancy regarded him, open-mouthed. 'Run away? Theo? Oh, but . . . When did this happen?'

He looked at her reprovingly. 'I can only read from my notes, ma'am.'

'I'm sorry. Please go on.'

'The police were notified and a search started. It was ex—' He glanced up apologetically. 'Can't read my own writing!'

Nancy pressed her lips firmly together. No point in alienating him.

The policeman went on, 'A search was started and it was expected that he would be close by. Mr Grey didn't want to . . . to alarm you so he waited a few hours. The boy wasn't found so—'

'So how long has he been missing?'

'His absence was discovered earlier this morning.' He turned another page. 'Mr Grey thinks he may be on his way home as the boy had some money and might have bought a something ticket . . . Oh! Train ticket.'

Nancy could hardly breathe.

She said, 'He's only nine. Where can he be? We must find my father. He's probably around the stables. Thank heaven he's not at the races. I'll take you down there.'

Nancy snatched an umbrella from the rack, gathered up her skirts and led him towards the stables. Once there a shock awaited her. Jack Liddy hadn't seen him all day.

'But that's not possible,' Nancy stammered. 'That is, he isn't in the house. I've looked. He must be down here – unless he's gone into town, and he wouldn't do that without telling me.'

125

The policeman said, 'Do I take it your father has also disappeared?'

He sounded hopeful, Nancy thought, annoyed. 'Of course not! Wait here with Mr Liddy and I'll—'

Liddy said, 'If he's gone into town he'll have taken the trap.'

'He won't have done,' Nancy told him, 'because Symes is at home with stomach trouble. His wife told me. Unless he's driven himself – and there's only one way to find out.'

She made her way back to the barn and tugged open the door.

'Papa! There's a policeman here about—'

The sentence was never completed. Her father lay sprawled against the hay bales. For a moment she imagined he was resting but almost at once intuition told her something was wrong. She moved a little closer and saw that his eyes were open. But he appeared not to see her.

'Papa?' Her chest grew tight with apprehension. 'Are you . . . ?' There was a small hole in his temple and a thin line of dark liquid had congealed on his cheek and stained his collar.

'Oh no!' she whispered. This couldn't be happening. 'You wouldn't do this, Papa!'

Then she saw the revolver beside him on the hay. For what seemed like an interminable time, she was enveloped by a terrible blankness until this was replaced by a great rushing sound inside her head. Her vision darkened and she knew she was falling.

When she came round she was on the floor of the barn. It took a few moments for her memory to function and then she raised her head and stared in disbelief at her father's body. How much time had passed? she wondered faintly. She was shivering with shock and as she struggled to her feet she felt the first wave of nausea. She took a few shaky steps towards her father but as she reached him her legs buckled and she sank to her knees beside him.

'Dear Papa . . .' she began but words failed her. Instead she took hold of his hands in a vain attempt to offer comfort and was shocked to feel how cold he was.

At that moment she heard voices behind her and turned to see Jack Liddy and the police constable silhouetted against the light from the doorway.

Liddy said, 'You all right, miss?' Then, 'Jesus Christ! It's the guvnor!'

Nancy said, 'I think he's dead,' and covered her face with her hands.

The two men came to stand beside her and she lowered her hands.

The constable, white-faced, stammered, 'Well now, this isn't looking good. Not good at all.'

Liddy stepped nearer and looked closely into James Franklin's face. 'Not looking good?' he muttered. 'It's looking ruddy terrible, that's what it is. The guvnor's dead. It's a ruddy calamity!' Gently he closed James's sightless eyes. 'Poor sod! Poor old sod!' he said.

At that moment the constable leaned down to help Nancy up. He said, 'Please don't touch anything, Mr Liddy. That's most important. Fingerprints – that sort of thing.'

Nancy stumbled to a sack of oats and sat down heavily on it. 'I can't believe it, that he's dead.' The sound of her voice, so changed, frightened her.

Liddy said, 'I'm afraid he is, Miss Franklin. He's gone for sure, God rest his soul.' He stared at the body, his expression somewhere between shock and horror. Then he crossed to her and patted her shoulder in a clumsy gesture of comfort.

The constable started to make notes. He took a watch from his pocket and consulted it and wrote again. Then he said, 'Did Mr Franklin have any enemies?'

Nancy and Liddy stared at him.

Liddy said, 'Enemies? He's shot himself, man! Anyone can see that.'

Shocked by his brusque words, Nancy put a hand to her heart. 'We don't know that,' she whispered.

At once Liddy touched her arm in a brief gesture of contrition. 'Forgive me, Miss Franklin. I spoke without thinking. I didn't mean . . .'

Nancy recovered slightly. 'Mr Liddy is right, Constable. Papa had no enemies. He – he did this to himself.'

The constable shook his head. 'We must never jump to conclusions, ma'am. This must be looked into carefully. Either way there is a crime involved. Suicide is against the law, as no doubt you know.' He studied his notebook. 'I shall have to use your telephone, Miss Franklin, and notify my sergeant. He may want to come up himself, this being a very serious business.'

Nancy nodded wordlessly. She was beginning to feel rather sick and very cold. Jack Liddy was looking at her with a worried frown. 'You'd best get some help, Miss Franklin. You shouldn't be alone after what's happened. Best call Mr Lawrence or his mother.'

'No! Oh no, not Lawrence!'

She had to get out of the barn, she told herself, but leaving her dead father seemed cowardly. And there was Theo to think about.

Liddy said, 'Why don't you get Cook to organise a brew-up for us while the constable gets in touch with his sergeant?'

'But we can't leave Papa.' The thought of abandoning him was unbearable to her. Although her common sense told her he was dead, she couldn't accept the fact that they could do nothing for him. Already she was blaming herself for not seeking him out earlier. When had it happened? she wondered. Was there any way she could have averted the tragedy?

'I'll stay here with your father,' Liddy offered.

'Thank you. You're very kind, and . . .' She drew a long, shuddering breath. 'And yes, tea. A pot of tea. That's a good idea.'

'You go on ahead, ma'am,' said the constable. 'I'll just finish making my examination. I'll catch you up. Won't be a tick.'

He bent over her father's body again and Nancy felt sorry for him. He was young and as shocked as any of them. Sweat beaded his forehead and his hand shook as he wrote. No doubt his training had failed to match the reality of the situation.

In a daze, she made her way back to the house and broke the news to Cook and Dora as gently as she could.

Cook began to cry, throwing her apron over her face and sobbing loudly. Dora sat down heavily, her face white, one hand pressed to her heart. She said, 'Oh, miss, whatever will you do?'

Nancy looked at her with dawning horror as she considered the future. What *would* she do? It was a nightmare. She was overwhelmed with a sense of loneliness. Who could she possibly turn to for help? Unbidden, John Brayde's image rose in her mind. Calm, sensible . . .

'I'll try and reach Mr Brayde,' she told them, 'but please make a large pot of tea and . . . and a few sandwiches. Food's always comforting.'

Red-eyed, Cook emerged from her apron, took out a handkerchief and blew her nose. 'I'm that sorry, Miss Franklin. It was the shock and the thought that . . . that this place . . . Well, that nothing goes right any more. Not since that woman left. But you're right. They'll need something to sustain them. We all will. I've got some potted shrimps and some cheese and pickle . . .'

Nancy went to the telephone in the hall and gave the operator the number, praying that John Brayde would be at

129

home. He was. Haltingly she explained what had happened but before she had finished he cut her short.

'I'm on my way,' he told her. 'You won't have to deal with this alone. We'll sort it out together, I promise you.'

Nancy hung up the reciever and sat down on the bottom step of the stairs. Her mind felt empty, as though everything useful in it had been removed. There was everything to think about and nowhere to start.

'And Theo!' she whispered. They mustn't forget Theo. She thought of John Brayde. Hadn't he said Lucy had run away from school? If so he would understand. He would know what to do.

While she waited for him to arrive she decided to tell Moira Callender. It would never do to let Dora blurt out the dreadful news. She stood up and began the slow ascent. I have to be strong, she thought. Somehow I have to stay calm and not lose control.

'And Lilian!' she gasped, clutching the banister for support. Someone would have to tell Lilian and then what would happen about Theo? Legally he might have to live with her. She forced herself up the remaining stairs and had reached the landing when another question entered her mind. Without her father, what would become of the stables?

Eight

Nancy sat in the kitchen with Cook and Dora, their hands clasped round mugs of tea. Cook and Dora were eating sandwiches but Nancy found herself unable to face food. The image of her dead father was fixed firmly in her mind and her thoughts reverted constantly to the idea that she might have been able to prevent his death. She had known that Carroway's death on top of everything else would have pushed her father close to despair. Expecting him to drown his sorrows, she had left him to it. But could she be blamed for that? If she had tried to stop him it was doubtful she would have succeeded and maybe he had needed the few hours' oblivion that the whisky offered.

She said, 'At least he'll never know that Theo has disappeared.'

Cook said, 'They'll find him, don't you fret yourself. He'll pop up somewhere smiling that funny little smile of his.' The memory of his smile brought tears to her eyes.

Dora looked from the cook to Nancy, wide-eyed with dismay at the accumulation of grief.

At that moment there was a ring at the front door bell and Nancy leapt to her feet. 'That might be Mr Brayde,' she told them and flew down the passage to open the door.

John Brayde held out his hands and Nancy clasped them.

'Miss Franklin, I just don't know what to say to you,' he told her. 'Sorry is so inadequate. Your father was a fine man and his troubles were not of his making.'

Nancy nodded, more tears threatening as a result of his kind words. 'We're waiting for a detective to arrive. The poor little constable was rather out of his depth. Lucky he was here, though. He had come to tell us Theo has run away from school.'

She drew him inside and Dora took his wet coat and hat.

'We'll be in the drawing room,' Nancy told her.

As soon as they were seated she said, 'They have to consider murder but it's almost certainly suicide. That means Papa won't be buried in consecrated ground.' She sighed. 'I suggested to the constable that it might have been an accident but he wouldn't listen and I know it's not very likely. I thought we might pretend . . . He said that would be perverting the course of justice. It must have been point-blank range and therefore self-inflicted – unless it was murder made to—'

'Murder?' He was startled.

Nancy nodded, shamefaced. 'Murder made to look like suicide. For a terrible moment I did wonder if they . . . but then I realised that no one hated him enough to do that.'

'No one *hated* your father,' he agreed.

Her voice trembled and she swallowed hard. 'I can't begin to imagine what this means to poor Theo. First his mother leaves and then his father dies. I suspect Lilian will take Theo now he has no father. She might even want to come back to Franklins.' She rolled her eyes, exasperated with herself. 'I dare say I sound like a hysterical female but . . . I'm so glad you're here. I didn't know who else to turn to.'

He frowned. 'Wouldn't the Wiltons have been willing?'

'I couldn't ask them.' She looked down at the handkerchief she was twisting. 'I've decided . . . I'm afraid Lawrence and I . . . You could call it a parting of the ways.'

'I see. At least, I think I do.'

132

'I feel he's let me, and all of us, down. His friendship with Donald Cooper . . .' She left the sentence unfinished and looked up slowly. John Brayde's expression was one of deep sympathy but there was something else in his eyes that she didn't recognise. 'I can't really talk about it because Lawrence doesn't know yet. I was going to write to him but I haven't had time. The day's been full of crises. I hardly know which way to turn. I'm still reeling, to be honest. I feel as though I'm in the middle of a storm. I'm afraid Lawrence Wilton is low on my list of priorities at the moment.'

'You know you can rely on me, Miss Franklin.'

'Thank you.' She looked around her, hardly aware of where she was. 'I'm still rather shaky.' Sitting back against the cushions, she sighed. 'I must get in touch with the funeral director and arrange—'

'There's no hurry,' he told her. 'The police won't release the – your father's body until after the post mortem and you'll have to await the coroner's verdict.'

Nancy realised with a start that she hadn't been listening. Her thoughts had reverted to her childhood, when her father had been the most important person in her life. Without a mother, Nancy had lavished all her affection on her beloved Papa. She was ashamed of the jealousy she had felt when he married Lilian. Then Theo was born and he too had taken up a large share of her father's attention – but she had loved him for the sweet person he was and had championed him against his mother when necessary. Now she and Theo had both lost their father and life would never be the same.

She regarded Brayde guiltily. 'Forgive me, I can't concentrate. I keep drifting into the past.'

'Happier times,' he suggested gently. 'The mind is giving you a short respite from the pressures of the present. I was simply saying that it's too early to worry about undertakers and the funeral. Let the police deal with everything.'

She nodded. 'I had to tell Nanny and it was such a shock

for her. I'll just run upstairs again and see if she's all right. She's very frail. I wonder if I can be spared for a few moments.'

'Certainly you can. I'll hold the fort for you.'

As she mounted the stairs Nancy felt a little of her strength returning. John Brayde was with her and she knew intuitively that he was a man she could trust.

Theo chewed the toffee with relish for he was hungry. He didn't much care for the lady sitting opposite him but she had given him a sweet and for that he was grateful. There was no one else in the carriage and he didn't like the way she stared at him but they would soon be home and then he needn't talk to her any more. Her questions made him nervous and he didn't like telling lies but he had to be careful.

'You sure you're eleven?' she asked. 'You don't look very big for eleven.'

'But I am.'

'And your ma's meeting you at the station?'

'Yes. She might be a bit late but I'm to wait for her to collect me. Or maybe Symes will come in the wagonette.'

'Who's Symes, then?'

'Our coachman, but he does the garden too and mends things when they get broken.'

'My! You are grand, Theodore.'

He nodded. The woman was wearing very old shoes and very old clothes and she was very old altogether. Almost as old as Nanny, he thought with awe. She had a live hen in a basket on the seat beside her which kept making funny noises and poking its beak through the basketwork.

'My father's James Franklin. He's quite a bit famous,' he said with a sudden urge to impress her.

'James Franklin? Never heard of him.'

'Does your chicken lay eggs?'

'I hope it will. I've just bought it this morning.'

134

'We have a small pond and ducks. They lay eggs. Lovely bluey-green ones.'

The train began to slow down. The old lady got up slowly and picked up her basket. The train stopped and Theo wrestled with the handle, which wouldn't open.

'Here, let me.'

Impatiently she brushed him aside, opened the door and climbed down on to the wooden platform. Theo felt at home immediately because he knew Mr Jones, the station master, and Mr Jones's cat Stripey, who only had one ear.

The woman followed him to the gate where Mr Jones was waiting.

'Master Theo!' he exclaimed, with obvious delight. 'Will your folks be pleased to see you!'

The woman said, 'You know him, then?'

'Course I know him.' He winked at Theo. 'I've had the police on to me this morning to keep an eye open. You wait here a mo. I'll be on the blower to your pa,' he said. 'He'll be that relieved to see you.'

He clipped their tickets but the old lady didn't go away.

'Says he's eleven,' she said. 'I thought he was a bit young to be travelling alone but he showed me his ticket so I thought—'

'Done a bunk from school!' Mr Jones told her. 'Problems at home, poor kid.' He looked at Theo. 'They've had the police out looking for you.'

Theo felt terrible when he heard that. Papa would be very cross with him, but at least he was home and he wouldn't have to listen to Tommy's lies and the other boys asking him silly questions about Mama.

He stroked Stripey who was perched precariously on the gatepost and wondered if the little goat had arrived yet.

Nancy had only been with Nanny for ten minutes when Dora burst into the room, smiling broadly.

'It's young Theo,' she told them. 'He's turned up at the station.'

Nanny cried, 'Thank the Lord!' and clasped her hands in prayer.

Nancy said, 'Oh thank heavens!'

'And the station master's getting a carrier to bring him home. Mr Brayde took the call and he's like the cat that got the cream!' She gave a little skip of excitement and cried, 'I must tell Cook. I wanted to right off but Mr Brayde said I was to tell you first so—'

Nancy smiled. 'Go on then, Dora. This is wonderful news!'

They watched the girl rush from the room and then Nancy put her arms round Nanny in a gentle hug.

There were tears in the old lady's eyes as Nancy released her but they were tears of joy. 'God is very good to us . . .' she began but then faltered as the loss of James Franklin resurfaced to dull her delight.

Nancy's own joy was dimmed by the problems still remaining. 'How will I tell him?' she asked. 'About Papa, I mean. And Lilian. Oh!' She put a hand to her head. 'It's too much for him to bear!'

Even as she asked the question she remembered that John Brayde was waiting dowstairs. He had been through so much. He would advise her.

'I must talk with Mr Brayde,' she said. 'I'll be up again before the day's over.'

Downstairs she was greeted by Brayde who clasped her hands delightedly.

'I notified the police that Theo was safe,' he told her. 'I hoped you wouldn't mind. The detective constable has arrived to examine your father and he has brought a police doctor. I'm wondering about Theo's mother. Did she know he was missing? If so she ought to be notified that he's safe.'

'The detective might know. I'll check.' She glanced out of the window, longing to see Theo safe at last but dreading the task ahead. 'How do I tell him about Papa?' she asked. 'If he sees all the activity down by the barn he'll know something is happening.'

Brayde joined her at the window. 'This is only a suggestion,' he said slowly. 'But would it help if he came home with me for a few days? Lucy would love to have some company and she's old enough to be discreet.'

Nancy thought about it. 'It might help. I'll see how he takes to the idea. I could tell him Papa has had an accident and is in the hospital. That would break the news one step at a time. When he has accepted that Papa is ill I could tell him he's died – in a few days' time, perhaps. And he's going to wonder where his mother is. I can't tell too many lies but perhaps I could say she is still staying with her sick friend. We really need to know what she is going to do about everything. In the meantime I shall have to stall for time.' She looked at him unhappily. 'I don't want him to feel he's being pushed out. He's very bright and he might know or guess more than we think.'

'You really do have a lot to cope with, Miss Franklin, but you'll do it. Believe me, the strength comes from somewhere.'

Nancy was startled by the tenderness she saw in his eyes. He understood and he cared. John Brayde was turning out to be a very valuable friend, she reflected, and wondered why there had never been closer relations between the families. But, of course, that had been a result of her father's oft-repeated maxim: never get too close to the owners. Training racehorses was a business like any other and he needed to keep a distance from his clients.

She was brought up sharply by the realisation that the future of Franklins was now in doubt. If her father had left the business to Lilian she might well put in a manager of some kind or even sell it. If Lilian sold it, claimed Theo and retired to Dorset to live with Cooper, Nancy and Moira Callender would be homeless. There was a large question mark over the future for all of them. Bitterly she blamed herself for never appreciating her comfortable life until it was about to be snatched away. In fact, she had been longing to get away from Franklins and start life anew with Lawrence, happily leaving her father and Theo behind her as she began her own family. Now she had lost everything – her past had gone and her future was whatever she could make of it. Without the security of a good marriage she would be adrift.

At that moment the rattle of the carrier's wheels and the clip-clop of horses' hooves announced Theo's arrival and the next few minutes passed in a rush of greetings, hugs and kisses. Tactfully, Brayde took himself off to the barn to see what progress the police were making which left Theo alone with Nancy. A delighted Cook organised a tray for Theo – scones and jam, cake and a glass of milk, and Dora brought it to him. While he was tucking in, Nancy did her best to appear calm and reassuring as she answered his questions.

'Why can't I go down to the stables? Does Papa know I'm back? Has Papa had any winners?'

The one thing he hadn't commented on was his mother's absence, she noticed. Perhaps he was afraid to ask.

Taking a deep breath to steady her nerves, she said, 'Mama is still with her friend in Dorset. We're not sure when she'll be back. She was worried about you when you ran away but now she's—'

'Has the goat come yet?' He bit into a second scone and jam and cream slithered off the scone and on to his shirt.

Nancy wiped it away with her handkerchief. 'It's due in a day or two. It's too young to leave the mother goat.'

How would she persuade him to stay with John Brayde if the goat arrived on time? She shook her head dazedly, deciding to worry about that later. 'And poor Papa has had a bit of an accident,' she told him.

He gave her a quick glance then fixed his gaze upon his scone.

'Did he fall off his horse?'

'No. He . . .'

'You did, didn't you?'

'Yes.' She stared at him. 'But that was years ago. Who told you that?'

'Mama told Mr Cooper and they laughed and he said, "The wrong kind of seat. Not like you," and then he patted her bottom. So what happened to Papa?'

She hadn't had time to invent the details. Stammering a little she told as few lies as she could. 'He fell down in the barn and . . . and banged his head. It was a particularly nasty bang so the doctor sent him to hospital for a little while.'

He picked up a slice of currant cake and began to pick out the currants, which he ate one at a time.

He's testing me, thought Nancy, shocked. He's not allowed to pick at his food. If I don't correct him he'll know we're treating him with kid gloves. Sharply she said, 'You know Mama doesn't like you doing that.'

'I'm sorry.' He glanced up at her. 'Tommy gave me a bar of chocolate. He said Mama has run away.'

'Theo!' She tried hard to hide her confusion. 'I – I hope you didn't listen to him. Some boys, even big boys, are very silly. *You* are the one that ran away. You gave us all a bad fright.'

'I don't like it at that school. Not any more.' He took a long drink of milk and said, 'I really wanted lemonade. Who's Dora?'

'She's a new maid – to help Cook. She's very nice.'

'So when will Papa be better from his accident?'

'We don't know. We have to wait and see. It was a very bad bump. Poor Papa.'

'Shall we go to the hospital and see him?'

'No! That is, not yet. Papa is sleeping . . . The doctor wants him to stay asleep for a while because then he won't be moving about and his head will get better.' Disconcerted by his direct gaze she amended, 'Well, we hope it will.' Lying to him was so difficult but his life was changing drastically and learning the truth might be too much for him.

'Shall I write to Papa?'

'That's a good idea. Maybe tomorrow.'

He slid from the chair. 'May I go down to the stables now?'

Caught off guard, Nancy grabbed his arm. 'Not today, Theo. Poor Mr Liddy is so busy without Papa to help him . . . I'm afraid he's rather short-tempered and I don't think he would want you around just at the moment.'

Please forgive me, Liddy, she thought. He was usually a very mild-tempered man but until she was sure her father's body had been removed and the police had left, she didn't dare allow Theo to go past the barn.

Theo pulled a face to show his displeasure but Nancy suggested that he go upstairs and see Nanny. She always had a sweet for him and he ran off without further protest.

Nancy went into the office and sat down wondering where on earth she should begin. She would have to notify the owners about her father's death and some of them would probably remove their horses fairly promptly, which might alert Theo. And ought she to telephone Lilian? And probably the bank manager – and their solicitor. The list was endless. She sighed heavily. What she wanted most was to break down and cry but she didn't dare begin. Once the tears rolled she would never stop them.

When the telephone rang it made her jump. For a moment she was tempted not to answer it but reluctantly she lifted the receiver from the hook.

The operator said, 'I have a long-distance call for you.'

It was Lilian.

'Is that you, Nancy?' The voice quavered slightly.

'Yes, it is.'

'The police have just left. They said James is dead. Killed by his own hand.'

'It's true, I'm afraid. I have just sat down to start the telephone calls.'

'Poor James. Poor dear man.' There was a pause. Was Lilian crying? 'I keep hoping he didn't suffer.'

'I don't think he did. It must have been instantaneous.'

Nancy was surprised. Lilian sounded genuinely distraught.

'I'll have to come home – at least for the time being.'

Nancy rolled her eyes. Lilian was the last person she wanted to see and yet the idea of having someone to share the responsibilities was tempting. She hesitated.

Lilian said, 'Do you hear me, Nancy?'

'I hear you. Theo is here, Lilian. He ran away from school because they were teasing him about you and Mr Cooper.'

Now I've said it, she thought, and at once regretted the harsh words. She had intended to add that Lilian was partly to blame for her father's death but now she couldn't bring herself to put it into words.

There was a pause. Then Lilian said, 'I tried to speak to Lawrence. I thought he should be with you, that you needed someone at such a time. But his mother hung up on me. No manners, some people. I never did like the woman. I suppose they know I left James?'

'I expect Lawrence told them. He's known all about it all along, hasn't he?'

Again Nancy was aware that she sounded shrewish but this was the first chance she had had to let Lilian know the strength of her feelings. Lilian had started a chain reaction which was destroying the Franklin family.

She heard Lilian's sharp intake of breath. 'There's no need

141

to adopt that tone, Nancy. I have to admit I'm pleased that before long you will be moving to the Wiltons'. The sooner you're married the better for both of us.'

'I may not be marrying after all,' Nancy told her. 'I'm sure you can guess why that is. As you've said more than once, the Wiltons are a very respectable family. The Franklins are not.'

Lilian was silent. Then she said, 'But are you sure? What exactly has happened between you and Lawrence?'

'Lawrence's devotion to you and Donald Cooper is something I can't admire. Helping you two to deceive my father was unforgivable. One way and another, Lilian, your behaviour is causing us a great deal of unhappiness.'

Silence fell again and Nancy took a deep breath. Perhaps she had said too much. If Lilian did return to Franklins they would always be at loggerheads but in her present mood she no longer cared. She said, 'Father's will should be interesting.'

'Why should it be interesting? I'm his wife.'

'But you left him for another man. He's had time to change his will.'

'Change it?'

It hadn't occurred to her, thought Nancy. In fact, it had only just occurred to Nancy herself and she was by no means sure that her father *would* have changed the will. 'We shan't know yet,' she added. 'It will be read after the funeral and we can't bury Papa until after the inquest. Come back to Franklins if you wish but nothing can be decided about the future. It will take some time.'

There was another silence and then Nancy heard Lilian speaking to someone – presumably Cooper. From the raised voices, Nancy assumed they were arguing.

Lilian came back on the line. 'I shall come up to Epsom as soon as I can. Tell Symes to stand by for a call from the station.'

142

'Symes is ill,' Nancy told her. 'In any case, Father has sacked him – for obvious reasons.'

'Then I'll come by carrier. I won't be bringing much luggage and I'll be alone.'

'I'm pleased to hear it. Donald Cooper will not be welcome here.'

'He doesn't want to come, welcome or otherwise. He has too much to do here.'

Nancy stretched her neck and shoulders which had tightened during their conversation. 'I've told Theo you're staying in Dorset with a sick friend and that Papa is in hospital after a fall. The poor lad's in for a terrible time and I'm trying to break it to him gently. Losing your mother and father in the same week is enough to destroy his young mind.'

'He hasn't lost me, Nancy.'

'That remains to be seen.'

Nancy wasn't at all sure what she meant by her cryptic comment but she hoped Lilian would find it unnerving.

At last Lilian said, 'You never did like me, did you, Nancy?'

'I tried to.'

'I don't think you did. I think you did your best to make trouble between me and your father.'

Nancy gasped. 'Well, if I did you probably deserved it!'

There was another silence. 'I gave up a lot to marry your father, Nancy. I didn't expect you to understand but I didn't expect such hostility from a child. Your father knew what you were up to but he had his work. I wanted to make him happy. To do that I needed to make you happy. I tried but you—'

'You tried to take him away from me!' The words came from the heart but even as she uttered them, Nancy knew they were untrue. Long before the marriage the young Nancy had decided that she and her stepmother would never be friends.

'Of course I didn't,' Lilian replied. 'James loved us in different ways. I didn't expect to replace your mother but I deserved some affection.'

'I couldn't love you.' To Nancy's horror, the childish words had a false ring to them. She had a sudden vision of herself lying face down on her bed with her fingers in her ears as Lilian gently remonstrated with her.

Lilian said bitterly, 'Did you ever try?'

Nancy didn't answer. She was seeing herself as a child, penning a note to Nanny. 'I hate her. I hate her. I hate her . . .'

'Nancy? Are you still there?'

Slowly, wordlessly, Nancy hung up.

The uncomfortable exchange had sprung from nowhere and had raised long-forgotten memories. Unhappily, she drew in a long breath. Her secure world was crumbling and now the past was coming back to reproach her. As she stared at the telephone she realised she was shaking.

Feeling the need for a few moments of reassurance, she decided to find John Brayde. The rain had stopped and the clouds were rolling back to allow the sun to shine. Brayde was deep in conversation with Jack Liddy and the two men glanced up as she picked her way across the puddled yard.

Brayde said, 'We're wondering if you would like us to continue racing those horses that have already been booked in. I don't suppose you've had time to think about that yet but it might be wise. You don't want to give the owners any excuse to move their horses.'

Liddy said, 'We might be able to manage for a week or two – that is, Mr Brayde's offered to lend a hand.'

Nancy looked at Brayde.

'Only if you wish it,' he said quickly. 'I certainly don't want to push myself forward.'

'And I don't want to ask too much of you,' Nancy told him. 'But it would be wonderfully helpful!'

The thought that he was willing to support her touched her deeply and she resisted the urge to throw her arms round his neck. John Brayde's generosity was making Lawrence's behaviour even more unforgivable. At the first sign of trouble Lawrence had backed away, encouraged no doubt by his parents. Why hadn't he talked to her? Why hadn't he tried to help? Presumably he had been too involved with Lilian and Donald.

Determinedly she pushed thoughts of Lawrence from her mind. Brayde and Liddy were right. The most important thing was to save the stables. Her father had invested his life in it and she couldn't let it go under. If the stables could be seen to be functioning as usual it might prevent panic among the owners. The news would be out within hours, she thought ruefully. From a racing point of view the disaster could not have occurred at a worse time for the flat racing season was in full swing and owners looked forward hopefully to their winnings.

She smiled at Liddy. 'I trust you both,' she told them. 'I know you'll do your best and I'm deeply grateful. All the information is in the office and we can go through it later on. But now, if you'll excuse me, I have to see Mrs Symes.'

Nancy found her in the garden, pegging out washing. A small boy played nearby with a wooden dog on wheels. He seemed to be chewing the animal's head and Nancy wondered vaguely if he was teething. He looked peaky and seemed unaware of the wet grass on which he sat. Nancy was immediately overwhelmed with a sense of guilt. She had never given the family a thought, assuming that Lilian or her father would have their welfare at heart. She, Nancy, should have taken an interest but she had been too wrapped up in her own affairs to spare any time for them.

Without preamble she said to Annie Symes, 'I expect you've heard that my father is dead.'

Annie lowered her hands. 'I'm that sorry, miss. Must have been a terrible shock for you. Finding him and that.'

Nancy nodded. 'Thank you. I can't imagine life without him, but . . .' She blinked back the tears that were never far away. 'I came to say that you can stay. Your husband's job is his for as long as he needs it.'

Annie's expression changed from despair to incredible relief at Nancy's words. 'Stay here? Oh, Miss Franklin! What can I say? George'll be so—'

'How is he?'

'Not so bad. They'll be sending him home tomorrow most likely but he's got to be careful what he eats. Lots of milk and jelly and that. Easy to digest. George won't like it, I'm afraid – he's a meat and veg man – but the doctor said an ulcer takes a long time to heal.'

Beyond Annie the cottage looked somewhat stark to Nancy's eyes. The windows needed cleaning and paint was beginning to peel from the back door. The garden was mostly laid to vegetables but there was a rickety hen house and a hutch from which several rabbits peered inquisitively.

Impulsively Nancy said, 'Is everything satisfactory inside the cottage?'

Alarm showed in Annie's face. 'Oh, miss, it's a bit untidy right now. I mean, you're welcome to come in and that but it's – it's not looking its best.'

'That's all right, Mrs Symes. I simply meant were there any outstanding repairs.'

'Oh, repairs.' She dipped into her basket again and pegged up a pillowcase. 'The damp patch in the small bedroom's still there but we've pulled the bed away from the wall.'

'I'll send someone to look at it,' Nancy promised. 'Remind me if nothing has been done by the end of next week.' She

146

smiled down at the baby who scowled and continued to chew the wooden dog.

'Is it all right for him to chew that? I was thinking about splinters.'

Annie Symes shrugged and picked up the empty washing basket. 'It's his teeth and that. I've got some stuff for his gums but I can't be giving it to him all day long. It's not cheap.'

'I think we've got an ivory teething ring somewhere that used to be Theo's. Would that help?'

'I'll give it a try.'

A minute or two later Nancy was on her way back to the house. She felt depressed by the Symes family but their plight had briefly distracted her from her own troubles and she was glad she had set the woman's mind at rest. She made a mental note to remember the damp patch and the teething ring. Once she had imagined having children of her own but now that she no longer wanted to share her life with Lawrence, children seemed a long way off. Which reminded her that she had meant to write to him. Now she changed her mind. She would tell him to his face. She would walk across the fields—

'Nancy! Nancy!' Theo was running towards her with a broad smile on his face. 'May I go to see Lucy for an hour or two? Mr Brayde says I may if you approve. She's got a bicycle and a dog and a treehouse and two guinea pigs, and a governess who can teach me too so I don't have to go back to school! May I go, Nancy?'

Smiling, Nancy bent down to kiss him. 'Of course you may. That's a splendid idea.'

He fell into step beside her, skipping cheerfully. 'There's a policeman by the back door. He wants to talk to you.'

'Oh!' She thought hurriedly. 'I'll be able to tell him you're safely home, won't I?'

John Brayde was also waiting for her. 'I took the liberty

147

of telephoning my daughter to suggest she entertains Theo for a while. I hope I did the right thing. My chap will bring her over in the trap and they can go back together.'

'Absolutely the right thing.' She smiled at him. He really is a dear, she thought with surprise, and wished Lawrence had been half as kind.

The detective constable told her that he had conferred with the police doctor and that they had ruled out accident or foul play as the cause of her father's death. That only left suicide, he told her regretfully, and the death certificate would be duly filed to that effect. Her father's body had been taken to the undertakers and the rest of the arrangements were up to her. She would need to speak with the vicars of various churches in and around Epsom to find one who would bury him. In a monotone the detective explained that by taking his own life James Franklin had broken one of the Church's rules and there were certain penalties. The vicar might agree to a very simple service but no bells. The headstone would have to be small and inconspicuous and the actual burial plot must be chosen in unconsecrated ground.

'To deter like-minded people, I suppose,' he told Nancy.

Too choked with tears to answer, she watched him go with something akin to loathing.

An hour later she and Brayde watched the two children disappear down the drive and Nancy breathed a heart-felt sigh.

Brayde said, 'Theo will enjoy himself and my house-keeper is there if needed.' He shook his head. 'You look exhausted, Miss Franklin.'

'Do you think you could call me Nancy?' She felt her face colour the moment the words were out. 'Oh dear! Maybe I shouldn't have said that.'

He was smiling broadly, however. 'I wanted to ask it but wondered if the timing was right. I'd love to call you Nancy if you'll call me John.'

148

She relaxed. 'Then, *John*, I think I need a small sherry, and perhaps I can tempt you into something stronger than tea. Let's retire to the drawing room and steal ten minutes' peace and quiet. I think we've earned that.'

She wanted to tell him about her conversation with Lilian. If her stepmother insisted on coming home, Brayde might be made to feel unwelcome. She had no idea how Liddy would manage alone.

Five minutes later, sipping her sherry, she said, 'I'm afraid Lilian might sell Franklins before it starts to go downhill.'

'But it's Theo's birthright, surely.'

'She might want the money – and anyway, Theo is only nine. A woman can't have a licence to train.' She frowned. 'Unless she marries Donald Cooper.'

John raised his eyebrows. 'What does he know about training horses? He gambles but that's about all.'

Looking into his eyes, Nancy found herself wondering how it would have been if they had been brought together in different circumstances – and before she fell in love with Lawrence Wilton. There was so much about him that she found attractive. His voice was gentle but firm and she liked to hear him laugh. He walked with a certain sureness that lacked Lawrence's arrogance and his courteous manners also impressed her. Not that Lawrence lacked manners, but he chose as friends men with whom Nancy could never feel at ease. Men who, she suspected, would mock women when they were together in an all-male group. Donald Cooper was one such man. What on earth did Lilian see in him? she thought, amazed that she found him preferable to her father. She sighed deeply.

'Nancy! You're miles away!' John told her.

It was the first time he had used her Christian name and she found it comforting.

'I'm sorry.' Impulsively she touched his hand. 'I'm glad you're here.'

'So am I.'

There was a pause and then they both decided not to add to their admissions.

Nancy said, 'I know it's very selfish but I was wishing we could be sitting here with our drinks without a care in the world. Will it ever be like that again, do you think?'

'Why do you think that's selfish?'

She sighed. 'I was down at the cottage earlier. Poor Mrs Symes had four children and another on the way and her husband is in hospital and there's a damp patch on their wall. Ever since then I've been thinking how unfair life is. How hard for some people.'

'Now it's hard for you, too.'

'Maybe I deserve it.' Her mouth trembled. 'Maybe it will never be the way it was.'

He gave a slight shrug. 'Maybe not, but I'd like to think I'll always be able to offer help when you need it. We all need someone.'

She nodded. 'It hasn't been easy for you. Did anyone offer help when you needed it?'

'I think so.' He considered, his head on one side. 'My mother was there, of course. She saw us through the worst of it.' He finished his drink and set down the glass. 'If it would help I could contact the owners for you. I could say I was acting for you because you were in shock from your father's death – which you are.' He leaned forward. 'You think you're coping but you do need help. I know from past experience. When my wife died I couldn't sleep or eat but I carried on with day-to-day matters, ignoring my mother's pleas that I should see the doctor. One day I broke down. I began to shake uncontrollably and couldn't stop crying. It was frightening.'

'Poor John!' She clasped his hands, appalled at the image his words conjured up.

'I don't want that to happen to you, Nancy. I can see

150

you're a fighter but you mustn't harm your health. I hope you'll forgive me but I took the liberty of speaking to your doctor. He's coming by later.'

Touched by his concern, Nancy found her eyes full of tears which spilled over. She tried to speak but nothing came out and suddenly the tears were streaming down her face. John moved closer, put his arms around her – and briefly kissed her hair. At that moment she felt safe but almost immediately the fears rushed in again and she clung to him, terrified of a future that she could no longer predict.

Nine

Nancy awoke the next morning to find the room bright with sunlight. It was a few seconds before she recalled the events of the previous day. The doctor had sent her to bed with a sleeping draught just after six and the clock on her bedside said twenty past ten. She lay there for a while expecting all the problems to rush back into her mind but all she could think of was John Brayde holding her in his arms and kissing her hair.

'Oh!' she whispered. 'Lawrence! I have to tell him.'

Suddenly the prospect of meeting him face to face no longer appealed. She would write to him after all. Sadly she was aware that her letter might come as a relief to him. It would certainly please his parents. He could hardly be seen to be jilting her at such a time but if she took the initiative he could put on a convincing show of regret.

There was a tap on the door.

'Come in.'

Dora came in, the usual broad smile on her face. Was she naturally cheerful? Nancy wondered. If so, she envied her.

'Cook said not to wake you because you needed the sleep. And Mr Brayde says you're to have breakfast in bed and not to worry. He and Mr Liddy have done the gallops and . . . um . . .' Frowning, Dora searched her memory for the correct words. 'And the morning rounds at the stables.'

'But where's Theo?'

Another frown. 'Um . . . Master Theo stayed the night with the Braydes and he and Lucy are having fun.'

At last Nancy smiled. 'Then I'll agree to breakfast in bed just this once. Ask Cook for some stewed apple, toast and marmalade.'

Lying back against the pillows, Nancy became aware that her tears the previous day had been beneficial. She felt less tense and the pressure at the back of her eyes had lessened. Expressing some of her grief had eased her troubled mind and she was grateful to John Brayde for helping her through it.

Unready to face up to the problems that still awaited her, Nancy thought about her father in happier times. She was not yet willing to face the memory of him in death and trawled for an early recollection of the two of them together. It had probably been her fourth birthday when, accompanied by her mother, she had been carried on her father's shoulders to discover her birthday present – a Shetland pony who was trying to eat the large blue ribbon tied round his neck. The stable lads had turned out in force to see her face and a ragged cheer greeted the moment when she first patted the horse's soft nose. She had been enchanted by the animal and within a few weeks was riding it around the grounds unsupervised.

'Monty!' she whispered.

That had been the horse's name. He was twelve years old and as docile as a sheep. She smiled again and now her mind threw up another image – that of her father at Doncaster racecourse, leading in Bad Lad, his tenth winner. She saw his face, flushed with success, and the modest smile as the horse's owner, dizzy with excitement, slapped him repeatedly on the back. Her father had searched the crowd for his daughter, wanting her to share in the moment. She had been eleven then and her mother was dead.

She sat up as the door opened and Dora staggered in with a laden tray.

'What's all this?' gasped Nancy as she saw bacon and eggs, mushrooms and tomatoes.

'Cook says you're to feed yourself up a bit. You're going to need it.'

With an attempt at professionalism, Dora removed the teapot to the bedside table so that it wouldn't spill on to the bed then stepped back proudly. 'Enjoy your breakfast, Miss Franklin.'

'Thank you, Dora. Have we confirmed that you shall stay with us?'

'Not yet, miss.'

'Then I think we should. Please tell Cook that if she is satisfied we'll consider it settled.'

'Oh, *thank* you, Miss Franklin.'

Nancy discovered that she *was* hungry after all and settled down to eat with a sense that maybe, just maybe, she would survive.

Writing the letter to Lawrence was much harder than she expected. She thought about it while she washed and dressed and then settled at her desk to write.

> Dear Lawrence,
>   This will be difficult for both of us, I know, but I think it has to be said. Cruel circumstances have come between us with unexpected results. What we once felt for each other . . .

It was hard now to recall just how much she had loved him. It seemed with hindsight that she had fallen in love for all the wrong reasons – he was handsome and came from a wealthy and well-respected family. And he adored her. They made a striking couple and everyone marvelled at the 'love match'.

She would marry him and bear his children. One big happy
family. It had all seemed so simple. So inevitable. The two
families met up at race meetings and invited each other to
dinner. Nancy had thought Lawrence the most wonderful
man in the world and was astonished at her good fortune.
Today, as she sat, pen in hand, she knew with real sadness
that the dream had ended. Fortunately, however, neither she
nor Lawrence would suffer a broken heart.

Perhaps Lawrence was not yet ready for marriage but
had been swept along by the tide of enthusiasm that had
engulfed them. She was thankful that she had found out in
time just how shallow his love for her had been. At the first
hint of scandal he had begun his retreat. Sighing, she went
on with the letter.

> What we once felt for each other has faded. I think
> we both accept that. It happens. It's a fact of life.
>
> I can't marry you, Lawrence, and you know why. I
> think in many ways this letter will come as a relief.
> Sad though it is, perhaps we can escape the bitterness
> that usually follows the breaking of an engagement. I
> think we should both be glad that we discovered our
> mistake in time.
>
> I'm returning your ring and now consider our
> engagement at an end. I will notify whoever needs
> to be told.

She thought with dismay about the vicar, the dressmaker,
the caterers, all of whom would have to be informed of the
cancellation. The young bridesmaids would be heartbroken,
their friends would be mortified. At least her father wasn't
alive to see her humiliation.

> The love between us can never be restored but we must
> try and remember the happy times and hopefully we

155

can remain friends. It just remains for me to wish you
and your family all the best for the future.

Very sincerely, Nancy

She almost added kisses but stopped in time. There was no
point in confusing him. Rereading the letter, she acknowledged to herself that it was far from perfect, but in her
present state it was the best she could manage. There were
so many things to deal with which took priority.

At the bottom of the stairs she turned towards the kitchen.
Cook and Dora looked up as she entered.

Holding up the letter she said, 'As soon as Dora can be
spared I'd like her to take this letter to the Wiltons'. You'll
both have to know sooner or later – I'm breaking off my
engagement.'

Cook, taken by surprise, said, 'Oh no!'

Dora clapped a hand to her mouth and stared, wide-eyed,
at Nancy.

Nancy said, 'It's for the best,' and laid the letter on the
table. She added, 'My ring is in there, Dora, so please don't
lose it. Cook will tell you how to get there.'

No one spoke as she hurried from the room but the sight
of their shocked faces accompanied her as she almost ran
to the office. There she intended to immerse herself in work
in an effort to forget the implications of what she had done.
Already she was wondering if she had been too hasty.

The telephone rang almost as soon as she sat down and
she reached for it eagerly. Anything to take her mind off
her personal problems.

It was Lady Millicent Deepny. 'I'm sorry, my dear, to
telephone with bad news but I know you will understand—'

'Oh, please! No!' cried Nancy who at once guessed what
was coming. 'I can assure you . . . At least give us a little
more time to—'

'Please don't try and change my mind. It's made up and that's an end to it. I cannot see how Franklins can possibly continue without your father. It's a question every owner is asking himself. You do understand that, I hope. No one is blaming you or saying anything about the management of the stables but without your father . . .'

Nancy was dumbfounded. The shock was total. She had feared this but it had happened so quickly. For a moment she couldn't speak.

'Miss Franklin? Are you there?'

'Yes, but . . . It's so . . .' She tried to swallow but her mouth was dry. At last she said, 'But shouldn't you speak with my stepmother before you decide anything?' It was a long shot but she was desperate.

'Speak to Mrs Franklin? I thought she had left Franklins.'

'She'll be home in a day or so.' Nancy crossed her fingers.

'Coming home? Well, that is rather unexpected. But what on earth does your stepmother know about training horses?'

'If the stables are left to her she may well—'

'She may do what she likes, Nancy. I wouldn't trust that woman near one of my dogs, let alone a horse!'

'I don't know what to say.' Nancy floundered. 'It's such a shock.'

'A shock? But I spoke at length to Mr Brayde last night. Hasn't he told you?'

'I haven't seen him today. The doctor made me take a sleeping draught and I was very late getting up. Lady Deepny, are you sure you—'

'Am I sure? Of course I'm sure. Goodness knows what is going to happen to Franklins. I'm sorry, naturally, but I can't take any more chances with my animals. And don't think this has anything to do with Carroway – although that was a tragedy that might have been avoided.'

157

'Oh, that's most unfair!'

'I did say "might". Hindsight is always rather cruel. No, it's self-preservation, plain and simple. Franklins may survive although I doubt it. I am not prepared to wait and see.' She stopped to draw breath.

'Lady Deepny, I beg you to reconsider!' Nancy's voice shook. 'If you would give us a week—'

'No, Miss Franklin, I won't. This call is to let you know I shall be sending a couple of horseboxes tomorrow. I shall of course settle my account and I should like you to send it promptly . . . I'm sorry about your father. Dreadful business. I don't know what he was thinking of to leave that poor child fatherless as well as motherless. I can't believe I trusted his judgement all these years!' She hung up.

Slowly Nancy replaced the receiver and sat staring into space. This was the beginning of the end. Where Lady Deepny led others would follow. By the end of the week the news would be out.

'A week!' she muttered. 'Just a week's grace.'

The desertion had shaken her to the core and she was still deep in shock when John came into the office. Immediately Nancy remembered her tearful breakdown and John's response to it. She stood up, feeling the colour rush to her face.

'Thank you . . . for everything,' she stammered. 'For fetching the doctor and . . . and making those calls. I felt much better when I finally woke up.'

He, too, looked slightly self-conscious, she thought. Was he remembering?

He began, 'Lady Deepny—'

'I've just been speaking with her.'

He shrugged. 'I did my best to reason with her but she was adamant. She won't be the only one, but Colonel Harding did promise to wait a couple of weeks. He's a decent old stick. He and my father were at school together.' He sat down on

158

the edge of the desk. 'Lucy and Theo are great pals. Getting on like a house on fire. Comparing notes about boarding school. Lucy's promised Theo a kitten when they arrive. I hope you don't mind.'

'Not at all. He's going to need something to love apart from the goat. It all depends on Lilian.'

'He keeps asking when she's coming back. He obviously misses her.'

'Well, she's coming back shortly, maybe tomorrow, but I don't know how permanent that will be. I don't think she knows herself.' She frowned. 'She can't abandon him now that he's lost his father. Can she?'

'It may depend on Cooper. If she has to choose between the two of them – who knows?'

Nancy frowned. 'I've been wondering whether to talk to her about him, but she may not want to confide in me. And I don't know what would be best for Theo. If Lilian stays with Cooper and they take Theo, will he be happy with Donald Cooper as a stepfather? I want to do the right thing.' She closed her eyes briefly. 'I want to do what's best for everybody, but—'

'Nancy!' He was shaking his head. 'Don't take all the responsibility on to your own shoulders. You may want to make everything turn out well but how can you expect to do that? You don't control everyone else. You don't know what any one person will do. If you expect to work miracles here you are setting yourself up for bitter disappointment and I'd hate to see you crushed.' He took hold of her hand. 'None of this is your fault, Nancy. You must remember that.'

For a moment she was silent. 'But I have to look out for Theo. He's all I've got.'

'Theo still has his mother, Nancy, and he loves her. She must have some feelings for him.'

Nancy's eyes flashed. 'How can you say that after what she's done to him?'

'So far she hasn't done anything – not in Theo's eyes. He still believes she's staying with a friend on a temporary basis and will soon be home. He's missing her but he's not aware of her defection. You've shielded him from that.'

'So far!' Nancy's shoulders sagged. 'Oh dear! I'm being difficult, aren't I. I should be looking on the bright side but I can't see one just yet.' Her voice shook.

'Have you got a date from the police yet for the return of your father's body?'

She brightened slightly. 'Yes. They've released it already. The verdict was suicide. But at least we can bury him. I have to talk to the vicar. He's very strict and I doubt if he'll allow much of a service but I'm going to plead for Theo's sake. He'll remember it all his life and I want a little music and flowers. He might relent.'

At that moment Dora popped her head in at the door and waved the letter Nancy had given her. 'I'm just off,' she announced. 'Cook says I should go now so as to be back in time for dinner.'

When she had gone Nancy looked at John. 'My final letter to Lawrence,' she said. 'A little overdue but final.'

His expression was unfathomable but he said quietly, 'I think you've done the right thing.'

'I can't quite believe it,' she confessed. 'How can love go wrong so easily?'

'Real love can't.'

She stared at him. 'So it wasn't love. Is that what you're saying?'

'Love is not love which alters when it alteration finds . . .' He smiled. 'I forget the rest but you know what I mean.'

'But all these years! I adored him.' She thought about it, frowning slightly. 'I built my whole future around him. My whole *life*!'

'Maybe you mistook admiration for love,' he suggested.

160

'I thought I loved him with all my heart.' Nancy still wanted to believe it.

'We all make mistakes,' he said kindly. 'You were very young when you first decided you loved him. Maybe you wanted to fall in love and persuaded yourself that here was a suitable man. You imagined it was the real thing. Romance. Isn't that what most young ladies long for?'

She tried to smile. 'So you're an expert on young ladies now, as well as horses?'

'There's no such thing!'

'Did you ever imagine you were in love?'

'I fell passionately in love with a parlourmaid when I was fifteen. That was romantic love.' He smiled. 'When she married the postman I was heartbroken. Later I met my wife. It wasn't at all romantic. She thought me a dull dog and I thought her a bit flighty. Over a year we adjusted our opinions of each other. I began to see her as vivacious, she began to think me sincere and reliable.' He smiled at the memory. 'We fought against falling in love until suddenly there we were, wanting to be together for the rest of our lives.'

'So there's hope for me yet!'

'I'm willing to bet on it.'

Nancy laughed. 'I don't find you at all dull.'

His voice softened. 'It's good to see you laugh.'

At his words she felt a jolt of guilt. 'I shouldn't be laughing at a time like this.'

John was shaking his head. 'Your father wouldn't want what happened to ruin your life, Nancy. It was a spur of the moment decision. A moment of dark despair. He certainly wouldn't have considered the results of his action or he would never have done it. If he could look down now he'd be praying that you and Theo don't suffer because of him. You will, of course, but you mustn't feel guilty about

161

getting on with your lives. That's what he would want. I'm sure of it.'

Nancy sighed. She was finding him easy to talk to but she must be careful not to pour out heart and soul. She *was* attracted to him; still, that didn't mean she should burden him with all her problems. It was time to change the subject.

'How's Jack Liddy coping?' she asked. 'I know you're helping him, but does he seem capable? He's never had to make the final decisions before. He and Papa settled things together.'

'He's taking The Genie to Kempton Park tomorrow. Your father had booked him in so Liddy offered to give it a try. It's his first race so he won't do anything but he has to make a start. Liddy will take one of the lads with him.'

'And you think they'll manage?'

'We have to try, Nancy. It's important for Franklins to be seen around. It won't look good if your horses suddenly disappear from view. The going should be soft after the rain but there's too much opposition. They wanted to familiarise the horse with the whole racing scene.'

'But suppose he wins? Shouldn't I be there? To represent my father.' As soon as she suggested it, she was aware of a frisson of fear. The idea of being the centre of attention was anathema to her.

Fortunately John was shaking his head. 'He won't win but anyway, his owner will be there.'

Nancy sighed. 'I suppose before long the news of Father's death will be out – if it isn't already.'

'You'll know by the reporters banging on your door asking for a quote!' He looked at her with compassion. 'It's going to get worse, Nancy. You have to be strong.'

'I know. I will be.' She spoke with more confidence than she felt but in a strange way her own words heartened her.

162

Perhaps she would find the strength of mind to carry her through.

'So give Liddy a chance,' John was saying. 'You're all going to have to accept changes and this is one of them. Now let's see . . .' He consulted the list again. 'We've withdrawn Trailblazer from Brighton. A shame really because Liddy fancied her chances on such a varied course. He says she does her best when faced with a climb and the home straight at Brighton is all rising ground. But we both thought we shouldn't press too hard at the moment. Two horses on the same day at different courses—'

'Concentrate our energies, you mean?'

'Exactly – but this is why you'll lose some owners. Everyone will know that it's not "business as usual" but only "the best that can be managed". Nothing personal, but where there's money to be lost and won people are naturally ruthless. They've paid good money for the horse and more good money for its training, feed, vet bills. The only way they can justify the expense is to see their animals win. They won't see them win if they aren't racing. If I didn't feel involved with you, Nancy, I'd probably be thinking of moving *my* horses.'

Nancy's first reaction was a spurt of resentment but she quickly forced back sharp words and acknowledged the truth of what he was saying. It also startled her to hear him say he was 'involved' with her personally. What did *that* mean? she asked herself.

She stood up, stretching awkwardly, aware of a knot in her back and the beginnings of a headache.

'John, would you like to stay on for a meal this evening?' she asked. 'I don't feel like eating alone.' With Lilian in Dorset, her father dead and Theo with Lucy, the prospect of a solitary meal was more than she could bear.

'I'd be delighted.'

*　　*　　*

As Nancy had expected, her interview with Reverend Blakely was not an easy one. She could see from his expression as soon as she was ushered into his study that he was unlikely to take a lenient view. With a stiff smile, he shook her hand then indicated an armchair and they both sat down.

He said, 'I've been expecting this "mission" ever since I heard the dreadful news of your father's death. It's a very sad business and you naturally have my condolences.'

'Thank you.'

As a young girl Nancy had been greatly in awe of him, unnerved by the flapping black vestments. Today she felt equally intimidated by him. There was a certain reserve in his manner which she put down to the circumstances and she found it difficult to broach the subject of her father's burial.

She said, 'It's been very hard for all of us.'

With a slight nod, he folded his hands in his lap. 'I remember your christening,' he told her. 'And that of Theodore. I also officiated at your father's first and second marriage. I think you will agree that the ties between us are close.'

It was Nancy's turn to nod. She clasped her hands and shivered, not only from nerves but from the coolness of the room, which was on the north side of the rectory. The lack of sun was compounded by sombre furnishings and the large windows were hung with thick lace and bordered with heavy satin drapes.

With an effort she straightened up in her chair. 'My father was in a state of deep depression when he . . .' Her voice wavered.

'When he took his life.' The vicar's grey eyes didn't falter. 'You would like me to give your father a normal burial, Nancy, but I cannot do that. I am bound canonically to bury all my parishioners who have been baptised—' he

164

held up a hand to prevent her interruption – 'except those who, though of sound mind, have laid violent hands upon themselves. I regret that your father comes into the second category.'

Though of sound mind. Nancy recalled her father's quiet desperation. Had he been in his right mind at the moment he pulled the trigger? She stared at Reverend Blakely, wondering how best to appeal to him.

He sighed. 'I can anticipate your next request,' he told her kindly, 'but the coroner found for suicide and I am bound by his verdict. It is not left to me to make a decision. I'm sorry, Nancy.'

'But there must be some way. Isn't it a matter for your discretion?'

'I fear not. To be precise, the ban on Christian burials of suicides applies to those persons who have reached the age of discretion and you must agree that your father had reached that age. A child or young person might be judged not to have reached the age of discretion, but—'

Nancy had no wish to hear more. She leaned forward. 'Then what exactly does it mean? I mean, what will there be in the way of a service?'

He hesitated. 'A silent burial.'

She stared at him. '*Silent?* Does that mean no prayers? No hymns? No bells?'

He shrugged. 'It was a mortal sin, Nancy. Nothing you say can change that. The taking of a life is a sin and must be punished. I'm truly sorry.'

'But who are you punishing?' she cried, her voice anguished. 'Papa is dead, so how will he suffer? You are punishing us, his family. You are punishing Theodore. What will he think if his father is buried in silence away from the other graves? He'll ask questions. Am I to lie to him?'

'You are blaming me, Nancy. I do not make the law but I must abide by it.'

'But who's to know?' she demanded. 'If we keep the date a secret and just the family attend . . . What harm is there in a hymn and a few prayers? Unless – would there be punishment for you if it were reported?'

'My punishment would be the pricking of my conscience,' he told her. 'Look, Nancy, we can find a pleasant plot for him and you may lay flowers.'

Nancy regarded him with growing dismay. She understood that as a minister he was bound by Church of England rules but her father had always claimed that some rules were made to be broken. Suddenly she remembered something Nanny had told her several years before.

'It does happen,' she told him. 'Moira Callender told me—'

'Ah, Miss Callender. How is she these days?'

'Rather frail, I'm afraid. But she told me about a young maidservant in Dunsbury who was caught stealing from her mistress. They threatened her with the police and so terrified the poor girl that she ran away and drowned herself in the river. Threw herself off a bridge. *She* was given a burial service. I remember that because Nanny was so impressed.'

He nodded. 'How very sad. But I cannot comment. It is always a matter of conscience.'

Another idea came to her. But how best to put it to him? 'Suppose that I write to the bishop and appeal to him. Would you feel able to conduct a simple service inside the church if the bishop took pity on us and authorised it?'

An awkward silence followed. Watching him, Nancy couldn't tell how he was reacting to the idea. He might well see that she was suggesting taking the matter higher, in which case he might be offended and refuse. But he had known the family a long time and she believed that in his heart he would want to help them.

He leaned back in his chair, frowning thoughtfully over steepled fingers.

At last he said, 'You are a very determined lady, Nancy. Very much like your mother in that respect.' To Nancy's surprise he smiled.

'My mother?' she prompted.

But he was not to be deflected. 'Suppose I contact the diocesan bishop on your behalf and explain the situation and your earnest request. I'll allow myself to be guided by him.'

Nancy felt a surge of hope. 'I'm forever in your debt, Reverend. Thank you so much.'

They both stood.

The vicar said, 'You realise that the answer may disappoint you.'

'At least I'll know we've done our best.'

As he led the way to the front door she paused. 'What did you mean about my mother? About her being determined? I remember so little about her.'

He smiled. 'Mrs Franklin was invited to join our Ladies' Committee just before Harvest Festival. After the service the time came for the offerings to be sorted into baskets and delivered. As you know people submit the names of worthy, needy recipients and your mother saw that Albert Jessop's name was missing.'

Nancy frowned. 'Would that be Mrs Symes's father?'

'Exactly.' He rolled his eyes. 'A terrible old reprobate, if the truth be known. And it was known. In previous years he had shocked so many of the ladies with his wild drinking and rude language that his name was never on the list. Mrs Franklin thought it wrong. She argued that he was old and poor and that made him eligible.'

Now Nancy was smiling.

'She persuaded them at last and his name was added to the list but then no one wanted to be the one to deliver the

167

basket. Your mother said she'd do it but she was expecting you so that was not considered quite proper. In the end Margaret Harding volunteered.'

'The colonel's wife! That was noble of her.'

'Wasn't it? I think your mother shamed her into it. In any case, apparently Jessop opened the door in his pyjamas, unwashed and smelling of alcohol. He saw the basket of food, nicely tied with a white ribbon, and realised he'd been put on the Harvest Festival list. He was so taken aback he didn't utter a single profanity, nor did he offer a "thank you". Instead he burst into tears and Margaret Harding, at a loss to know what to say or do, made good her escape. But here's the best bit. The next Sunday he appeared in church, all spruced up. First time ever.'

'So was he reformed?'

'Hardly.' The Vicar smiled. 'He only came once, but somewhere in the story is a Christian message for us all.' He shook Nancy's hand. 'You're your mother's daughter, Nancy. You can be proud of that.'

Two days later Lilian received a telephone call from Nancy. As she held the telephone she could see the Dorsetshire farmland in its early summer beauty and felt the familiar weight of disappointment. They had chosen this house for its quiet location and beautiful views and she had looked forward to sharing it with Donald. She had hoped they would grow old together here. Theo would look upon it as a second home and would spend his holidays with them. She had risked so much for that glimpse of happiness, but James's death had put an end to all that.

After a brief conversation she replaced the phone and turned to face Donald. He had finished his breakfast and was reading *The Times*.

'Did you hear any of that? My side, I mean,' Lilian asked.

'I wasn't listening,' he replied without lowering the paper.

Lilian ignored the snub. 'James is being buried tomorrow. The coroner's verdict was suicide, but the vicar has agreed to offer a short service in the church.'

Donald lowered the newspaper. 'He can't do that. It's against canonical law.'

'Well, you're wrong. He can and will do it. The Reverend Blakely applied to the diocesan bishop and was granted a special dispensation. I shall attend, of course.'

'I shan't. I'm not a hypocrite.'

'Meaning I am? I'm still his wife, Donald, and—'

Donald lowered the newspaper and peered over it. 'You're his *widow* and you walked out on him.'

'Widow, then.'

'You're a scarlet woman!' His glance was faintly mocking. 'They may not want you there.'

'I must attend for Theo. And I'm not completely hard, Donald. I want to pay my last respects.'

He shrugged and Lilian was aware of an unwelcome irritation. She loved this man but he was distancing himself from the unpleasantness of James's death when what she needed from him him was sympathy and understanding.

She went on, 'Also there's the will. I need to be there for the reading. I'm glad you're not coming. It wouldn't be suitable.'

He turned the page. 'Please yourself, dear. I never liked the man.'

'It was mutual . . . And Theodore will expect me to be present, poor little chap.'

Sighing, she poured herself another cup of tea and sipped it thoughtfully.

'We have to think about Theodore now,' she said. 'He has no father. He needs someone.' She waited for him to

169

comment but he was pretending to read. 'He needs me, Donald. Things have changed.'

Donald crumpled the newspaper and threw it down. 'He doesn't need you, Lilian. Don't fool yourself. He's perfectly happy without you. You told me he would be, remember? He has Nancy and Nanny. What more does he need?'

'Nancy is getting married.'

'She isn't, remember? It's definitely off. I had a call from Lawrence while you were in the garden. Nancy is not marrying Lawrence. In fact, she's not marrying *anyone*. She's going to look after Theo. So can we put an end to this pointless wrangling?'

Lilian looked at him unhappily. 'Poor girl. She absolutely adored the man. Surely they'll make it up.'

He shrugged. 'According to Lawrence, Nancy thinks he betrayed her. She doesn't trust him any more. Satisfied?'

Lilian put down her teacup and saw that her hands were trembling.

'Wasn't Lawrence awfully upset?' she asked.

'Naturally. Although I suspect he was glad of the opportunity to be free of the Franklins. His parents were doing their best to influence him. Now Nancy's backed away and that leaves Lawrence looking like a victim instead of her.'

'Didn't he love her?'

'For heaven's sake! How should I know?'

Lilian took a deep breath and decided to change the subject. 'I think James will leave the stables to me. If he does you and I could run it. Couldn't we?'

Donald pushed back his chair and stood up. 'I know damn all about racing horses and you know it. You know even less. How do you suppose we'd manage to train the damned horses? We'd be laughed out of town.'

She didn't answer.

Donald walked to the window and stared out. 'This is our home, Lilian. You wanted me to buy it and I did. I bought it for you and for our future. We agreed that Theodore wasn't to be a part of it. We can have a child of our own, if that's what you want, but don't ask me to bring up James's son because I won't do it. He's too much like his father. A damn great chip off the old block! Precocious—'

'He's bright . . . and sensitive.'

'Always on the sidelines, snooping around.'

'That's not fair. He's away at school most of the time.'

'He doesn't like me and he makes it obvious.'

'He's just a child, Donald.'

'No one's denying that but we agreed he wouldn't live with us.'

Lilian narrowed her eyes. 'You insisted, if I remember rightly. But things have changed. His father's dead and Theo needs me.'

'Well, go to him. Who's stopping you? But I'll tell you this for free—' He turned from the window, his face grim. 'You'll never make a go of Franklins, with or without me. You'll end up selling it and then you'll have nothing but your precious Theodore. Don't come whining to me when that happens, Lilian, because I won't be waiting for you. If you leave me now—' He closed his mouth ominously.

'Are you threatening me, Donald?' Suddenly her eyes were bright with tears. 'After all we've been to each other—'

Relenting, he went to stand beside her and pulled her none too gently to her feet. Staring into her face, he said, 'I thought you wanted to be with me. You said nothing would come between us. That's the way I want it, Lilian. Just you and me. Don't throw it all away. That's all I ask.'

She tried to answer, to reassure him, but he kissed her hard on the lips to silence her then stalked out of the room.

Ten

O n the morning of the funeral Nancy was awakened
from sleep by an urgent whisper from Theo.

'When is she coming, Nancy? When is Mama coming?'

Nancy sat up, only half awake, and looked at the clock.
'Theo, it's not six o'clock yet. Mama won't be here for
hours. Go back to bed and finish your sleep. I'll wake
you—'

'But I want to get up now, Nancy. She might come early.
Do you think she will?'

Nancy rubbed her eyes and pushed back her tousled hair.
The sight of Theo in his blue pyjamas melted her heart and
she held out her arms to him. 'Cuddle in with me for a few
minutes,' she urged, 'and then we'll both get up.'

'She will come, won't she?' Theo demanded, climbing up
into the bed and sliding between the sheets. 'Nanny says she
will because poor Papa is to be buried and she wouldn't stay
away for that.'

'Of course she'll come,' Nancy assured him although
she was still unsure. Lilian had sounded very odd on the
telephone. Very abrupt. When Nancy asked whether or not
she would attend, she had said, 'Probably.' But she must
guess that a reporter from the local newspaper would be
there and it would look very bad if James Franklin's widow
was not at the graveside. Knowledge of the suicide was
widespread and had aroused plenty of interest. Nancy had
hoped for a modest, private burial but this seemed unlikely.

172

The news was out that the bishop was allowing a certain leeway in the way of a service and already several people had lingered to watch the gravedigger at his sad task in a neglected corner of the churchyard.

A simple iron cross marked the only other grave and on the metal the name of Steven Pye had been scratched alongside the dates 1878–1899. Nancy wondered what had driven that unfortunate to kill himself and how he had set about it but had been too depressed to enquire. And what had *he* been given in the way of a Christian burial? All she knew was that Steven Pye and her father would have the untended area of the churchyard to themselves.

Now, with Theo beside her in bed, Nancy tried to prepare him for what was to come. He already knew that his father had died from his 'accident'. Nanny had volunteered to break it to him gently and Nancy had gratefully accepted her offer because Nanny had told *her* when her own mother died.

'You remember where *my* mama is buried, don't you, Theo?' she asked gently.

'Under the big stone,' he answered, snuggling against her. 'Next to Grandpapa and Grandmama. Is that where they will bury Papa?'

'No, Theo. Papa wanted somewhere quiet and we've chosen another place for him. It's near a nice tall tree and we'll plant a rose bush for him.'

Theo thought about it. 'Does Papa like roses?'

'Yes, he does.'

'Doesn't he like marigolds? I like them.'

'Well, we'll plant some marigolds as well. Or, better still, you can sprinkle the seeds and we'll watch them grow.'

'Why is it noisy where your mama is buried?'

'It's not noisy, exactly, but there are so many other graves and people going to and fro and—'

'And the man cutting the grass and sweeping up the

173

leaves. He's noisy. He always whistles. I've heard him. I asked him why he was whistling and he said, "Tis summat cheerful to keep away the ghosties!"'

'There you are then. Papa once said that he would like to be buried somewhere very quiet.'

Theo looked at her doubtfully. 'But he likes horses and they aren't quiet. Will there be horses in heaven?'

'I don't know. Maybe not. Maybe—'

'But where did Carroway go when he died?'

'Maybe to a special heaven for horses. We don't know a lot about heaven, Theo. It's a surprise. When you die you find out all these things.'

'Where will Thunder go when he dies?'

'Thunder's a toy horse. He isn't alive so he won't die.' Nancy was beginning to feel somewhat beleagured but Theo hadn't finished.

'And Mama? Does she like quiet places?'

'I dare say. I'm not sure.'

He glanced at the clock, studying the position of the hands. 'Now it's ten past six. Mama will be here any moment.'

'No, Theo. She'll just be waking up and she has to have her breakfast and then get on a train.'

'But she *is* coming, isn't she?'

'Of course she is.' Nancy gave him a hug and kissed the top of his head.

'She hasn't had an accident, has she?'

'No, Theo. In a few hours you will see for yourself.'

She realised with a sigh that he would never go back to sleep so reluctantly she threw back the covers. 'Let's get up, then, Theo,' she said and immediately he was out of the bed and racing down the stairs to find Dora and ask for the hot-water jugs.

An hour later, across the fields, Lawrence was entering

the breakfast room at Mannington Farm. He was nervous, anticipating a scene.

His mother, Amelia, glanced up from her stewed prunes. 'Had a bad night, dear?' she asked.

'Every night is a bad night,' he answered. 'I'm not sleeping at all well.' He helped himself to scrambled eggs and kidneys and sat down opposite his mother.

She said, 'What is it, Lawrence? I know that look. Something's—'

'I'm going to the funeral, Mother. I've made up my mind.'

'To the funeral? Oh no! Whatever will your father say? We decided against it, dear. For everyone's sake.'

'Hardly everyone, Mother. I don't think we considered Nancy's feelings when we came to our decision.' He stared at his food, picked up his knife and fork and then set them down again. 'How is she going to feel seeing an empty church? I feel she needs support, Mother, not ostracism.'

'Ostracism? Now that's a ridiculous word to choose!' She looked at him indignantly. 'Your father had no intention of ostracising her. He merely thinks it more suitable – for her sake. We should allow her to bury her father in peace. It's a shameful thing to have to do – to bury a suicide. She doesn't want an audience. In her shoes I should want to lay him to rest in decent privacy.'

Lawrence sighed. 'I don't really believe that, you see. I thought about her during the night and I think she might appreciate some support from her friends.'

'Your breakfast is getting cold.'

'I'm not really hungry.' To disprove this remark he scooped egg on to his fork and swallowed it.

At that moment his father entered the room. Harold Wilton was a tall, red-faced man with white hair and a small moustache. He had dressed but wore his dressing

175

gown over his clothes. Amelia looked at him in surprise. 'You're late, Harold.'

'The damn water was cold. I had to send down for some more.'

'It was hot enough for me.'

'Maybe, but I must have dozed off again. Morning, Lawrence.'

Before Lawrence could answer, Amelia rushed in with news of her son's change of heart.

Harold reached for the toast. While they waited for his response, he carefully buttered the toast and spread marmalade. Then he said, 'Not the thing to do, Lawrence. Not the thing at all. They're nothing to do with us now.'

Lawrence's chin jutted. He had done a great deal of thinking during the long night and had reluctantly come to the conclusion that he was often too easily influenced by his father; too ready to be advised by him, in fact. His mother rarely argued with her husband and Lawrence had unconsciously copied her example. James Franklin's funeral was a case in point and Lawrence was going to break with tradition.

'It's nothing to do with Nancy,' he began. 'It's a—'

His father's head snapped up. The pale blue eyes stared into his. 'Of course it is. He's her father. James Franklin has brought shame on the family and you're well rid of them. He's committed a sin and he's being punished for it. There is absolutely no reason for us to stand by and watch.'

Amelia reached out and patted Lawrence's hand. 'Be guided by your father, dear. He knows what's best for you. For all of us.'

'I'm not interested in *us*,' Lawrence insisted. 'I want to be there for Nancy – and for James Franklin. We always got on well together. Dammit, I *admired* the man.'

Amelia frowned. 'There's no need to use that kind of language, Lawrence. And think what Nancy did to you. She

returned your ring. Broke off the engagement. I hardly think
she deserves our support.'

'Or anybody else's!' Harold glared at his son.

Lawrence bit back a sharp rejoinder. Anger was replacing
his nervousness. 'Nancy broke off the engagement because
I . . . because I let her down over Donald Cooper. She had
a point. I can see that now.'

Harold snorted. 'Don't mention that bounder to me! You
should never have encouraged it. And then there's Lilian.
She might be there. And the Cooper fellow. How do we deal
with them if we come face to face, after all that's happened
in the past weeks?'

Amelia stared at Lawrence, visibly shaken by her husband's words. 'You don't think they will come, surely? Oh
dear! How very difficult.' She turned to Lawrence. 'I really
do think you should stay away, dear. It's going to be a very
nasty affair.'

'Maybe,' he admitted. 'But that's all the more reason why
Nancy should have someone there to help her. I'm going, so
there's nothing more to be said.'

'On your head be it!' his father muttered. 'Just don't come
running to me when it all blows up in your face. And don't
start things up again with Franklin's daughter.'

Lawrence pushed away his plate. 'Franklin's daughter?
Franklin's daughter! Her name's Nancy, in case you've
forgotten, Father!' He stood up. 'And if I wanted to "start
things up", as you put it, I would, although I very much
doubt that she'd be willing. But that's not the point.'

His mother said, 'Please don't raise your voice, Lawrence.
Your father is only—'

Lawrence appeared not to have heard. 'James Franklin
was a friend. He was going to be my father-in-law. You and
Mother spoke very well of him and you wanted the marriage
as much as we did. James Franklin always treated me very
well and I returned his trust by conniving with Donald and

177

Lilian. If you must know, I feel partly to blame for what happened. For what he did.' His voice was shaking as he pushed back his chair. 'The least I can do is show some respect at his funeral.'

By the time the mourners gathered in the church the day had turned cool with a fresh wind. Nancy sat beside Theo who, resplendent in a new dark navy sailor suit, sat silent and still, clutching his small wooden horse. Nanny, her eyes closed in prayer, sat on her other side. Lilian had not arrived.

James Franklin's coffin rested on a wooden trestle set before the altar. A simple arrangement of roses lay on top of the polished mahogany. The family had had no chance to view the body in the casket, as it had come straight to the church from the undertakers. Nancy had felt unwilling to see her father again but now she saw that Theo cast occasional glances at the coffin.

'I want to say goodbye to Papa,' he whispered suddenly, nudging Nancy's elbow. 'We said goodbye to Grandpapa.'

Nancy groaned inwardly. She had been hoping to avoid that particular request. Her own memory of her father's body on that last fateful day still lingered starkly in her mind. He had also undergone the indignities of a post-mortem examination but Nancy had steadfastly refused even to think about that. She had no idea how well the undertakers had dealt with her father's body and had been more than willing to forgo the normal, formal viewing.

However, Theo was only nine and maybe his memories would fade faster if he didn't see his father now. Uncertain, she looked at Nanny for guidance and, after a moment's hesitation, the old lady nodded.

'Better let the lad see his father one more time,' she whispered.

Telling Theo to stay with her, Nancy hurried out of the church to find Mr Darren, the undertaker, waiting beside the carriage, which was sombre in its black drapes. He had made no argument about providing a coffin for a suicide and had spoken respectfully of her father throughout their meeting. Now he touched his hat to her then listened politely to her request.

'The coffin's fastened down, Miss Franklin, but 'twill only take a moment to lift the lid. 'Tis only right the lad should see his pa. 'Tis only proper. Your father looks real handsome, Miss Franklin, though I say it as shouldn't. We hid the damage and did a few repairs, like. Our Master Hart is an artist in that respect. You've no need to worry on that score.'

He followed Nancy back into the church and bent discreetly over the coffin. In moments he had raised the lid and stepped quietly to one side. Nancy drew Theo from his seat and led him forward.

'Papa?' Theo stared in at his father.

James Franklin rested peacefully amid ruffled white satin and Nancy caught her breath in surprise. He looked almost alive. There was natural colour to his cheeks and, apart from looking tidier than usual, he looked entirely recognisable. Somehow Master Hart had minimised the damage inflicted by the gun and Theo would never guess that the back of his father's head was missing.

'I'm so sorry you're dead,' Theo began in a conversational whisper, 'but Nancy has found you a very peaceful place.' He waited a moment, then turned to Nancy. 'Can he hear me?'

'Yes, Theo. I'm sure he can.'

Theo turned back to his father. 'I'll come and see you in your peaceful place . . . and Papa, I know there won't be any horses in heaven so I thought you'd like Thunder to keep you company.'

Before Nancy could stop him he had laid his wooden horse in the coffin. She glanced doubtfully at the undertaker but he stepped forward and said softly, 'A very kind thought, Master Theo,' and gave Nancy a small nod.

Theo continued, 'You gave him to me, Papa, remember, when I was little, but I'm big now.'

Nancy felt tears pressing against her eyelids. 'Oh, Theo,' she whispered.

Theo said, 'Goodbye, Papa,' and turned cheerfully to Nancy. 'Now you say it.'

In a choked voice, Nancy made her farewell and they returned to their pew. Mr Darren closed the lid and withdrew and Nancy, relieved, was left with her thoughts. There were no choirboys and no one sat in the organist's seat. No bells would be rung. A quick glance had showed her the faithful few – George and Annie Symes, three of the stable lads and Cook – who had arrived early. Dora was finishing the last of the simple refreshments and Jack Liddy was at Aintree. How ironic it would be, Nancy reflected, if her father's burial was celebrated by a win.

Theo turned round repeatedly in search of his mother and suddenly he gripped Nancy's arm.

'Nancy! Nancy! Mr Wilton is here!' he told her.

Astonished, Nancy turned and caught Lawrence's eye. He was standing uncertainly at the back of the church as though awaiting permission to join them. She smiled and saw relief in his eyes. He took a seat at the rear of the pews and knelt to pray.

'Is he our friend again?' Theo asked loudly and Nancy was trying to hush him when he spotted another arrival.

'At last!' he shouted. 'Here's Mama!' He leapt from his seat and ran up the aisle towards Lilian who held out her arms to him. Nancy watched them embrace, a lump in her throat.

Nanny said, 'Lilian? About time too!' then lowered her voice. 'I thought you said she wasn't coming.'

'I said I doubted she'd come alone. When I spoke to

her I made it clear that Donald Cooper wouldn't be welcome.'

'Well, at least Theo's happy. Bless his heart. But where
should she sit?'

Nancy was wondering the same thing but after a moment's
indecision she stood up and walked to meet her stepmother.
'Please feel free to join us at the front,' she said. She
wanted to smile a welcome but her face was stiff and
unresponsive.

'If you think so . . .'

Lilian looked nervous, thought Nancy. She had no doubt
been wondering what sort of reception she would get from
the rest of the mourners. Unexpectedly Nancy felt a pang
of pity for her. Lilian was impeccably dressed as usual but
in black which set off her fair hair and blue eyes. Her
dress was trimmed with soft grey lace and there was a grey
feather around the brim of her hat. She makes a very striking
widow, Nancy thought bitterly, but noticed that Lilian's face
revealed the strain she was under. She was thinner and there
were telltale circles below her eyes. As Lilian and Nancy
passed back down the aisle heads turned in their direction
and there were murmurs of surprise and one or two muttered
comments.

'The cheek of it!'

'Would you credit that! As bold as brass!'

If Lilian heard she gave no sign and sat down in the front
row after a brief, 'Hello, Nanny.' Nanny gave a small nod
in return.

A delighted Theo sat between Nancy and his mother
and his childish chatter gave them all a chance to settle
themselves. The walk up the aisle had given Nancy a
chance to see who else had arrived. John Brayde was
there with Lucy, who gave her a quick smile, and Lady
Deepny was also among the mourners. She sat with David
Evans the vet.

181

Nancy hadn't expected to see Colonel Harding and his wife. They had already sent their excuses – they had visitors and were going to watch Cocksparrow run at Aintree. Nancy had agreed that maintaining a presence for Franklins was a priority for all those concerned in the stables. If the horse won, the owners should be there to be seen and interviewed.

A young man, who looked vaguely familiar, was busy with his notebook and Nancy realised with a shock that he was a reporter from one of the local newspapers. Most likely the racing page, she thought.

She was thankful when the vicar appeared and read a short prayer. They then stood to sing 'Rock of Ages' but it was a miserable, embarrassed rendering with so few voices and no music to give them courage. When the vicar went up into the pulpit Nancy clutched Nanny's hand, as much for her own comfort as for the old lady's.

'Dearly beloved brethren,' he began. 'We are here to lay to rest our friend James Albert Franklin. In life he was a good man, a loving husband to Lilian and a loving, caring father to Nancy and Theodore. He worked hard and deserved his success. His end was tragic but God, too, is a loving Father and forgives our sins. James Franklin will be sadly missed. We shall bury him with a prayer in our hearts and we will remember him with compassion.'

Short but to the point, thought Nancy, but he hadn't wanted to do it and she must be grateful for small mercies.

He glanced down at Nancy. 'We shall say the Lord's Prayer as the coffin is lowered into the ground.'

She nodded and watched with a tightness in her throat as he descended the steps and led the way out of the church. Four bearers from the undertakers lifted the coffin and carried it out.

At the graveside Nancy watched through a blur of tears, her throat tight with regret and loss. Theo clung to his

182

mother's hands but watched dry-eyed as the coffin was lowered into the ground. The vicar murmured something in Latin and it was all over. Without the bell the silence seemed oppressive but Nancy was concerned about Nanny who was very unsteady on the rough grass.

The old lady tugged at Nancy's arm and whispered, 'Not even a tear from his wife!'

It was true. Lilian's head was high and there was something akin to defiance in her manner as she observed her husband's burial. She appeared unmoved but Nancy refused to believe that she felt nothing. If her love for her husband had withered she should at least feel guilt for the part she had played in his collapse.

Nancy glanced around at the untidy surroundings. At least the yew tree was a good size but a few flowering shrubs would soften the impression of neglect. She would ask for permission to plant a rhododendron, she decided. Or better still, she would plant them secretly since it was unlikely anyone would notice the slow-growing plants. Perhaps the family would be allowed to present a seat to the churchyard – one which bore her father's name. She would speak to Lilian about it later.

Busy with her thoughts, she was startled to see that the vicar was now halfway back to the church and that the little crowd was dispersing. She caught Theo's eye and smiled. She hoped that, for him, the worst was over.

The solicitor was brief and to the point. He opened the document that was James Franklin's will and looked quickly round the table. Nanny was present with Lilian, Theo and Nancy.

Mr Scott cleared his throat. 'This is a very recent will,' he told them. 'My client came into the office two days before his death and made several changes. There were two witnesses, both members of our staff.'

Nancy did not dare look at Lilian. The solicitor's meaning was obvious. His wife's betrayal had caused her father to think again. If Lilian had hoped the original will was still operative, she was to be disappointed. Theo whispered to his mother but she put a finger to his lips and he fell silent.

'To whom it may concern, being of sound mind, I, James Franklin, make the following provisions for my family . . .'

No one spoke as the words rolled over them. James had left the stables to Theo. He had left five hundred guineas to Nancy. The house was also left to Theo and Nancy but Lilian, as Theo's legal guardian, was to be allowed to live there until Theo's twenty-first birthday. Financial provision would be made separately for both her and the running of the house. After Theo reached twenty-one, Lilian could continue there only if he and Nancy so wished. If Lilian married again at any time she relinquished all rights to habitation and the financial settlement would be withdrawn. Donald Cooper was never mentioned by name but James's intention was clear. Cooper was never to be part of the family. Nanny was to be provided for until her death and was left a small legacy of ten guineas.

In spite of the solemnity of the occasion, Nancy hid a smile. Her father had been very clever but she suspected he had acted more in sorrow than anger. He loved Lilian in spite of her faults and he could have left her destitute. Lilian would no doubt be aware of that, also.

It was perfectly clear to all those present that James had been very much in control of his wits and there could be no appeal. Nancy glanced at Lilian who was very pale. Her husband had left her an awkward choice and she knew it. She could stay on at Franklins as a widow and bring up her son or she could marry and lose her home and the lifestyle that went with it.

The solicitor folded the will and looked up. 'Does anyone have any questions?'

Nancy shook her head. 'No, thank you.'

She understood the will perfectly. She and Theo jointly owned the house and Theo owned the stables. That was fair in her view. Her brother had always stood to inherit. Theo would eventually have a family of his own to support. She, Nancy, would marry and be provided for by her future husband, whoever that might be.

Lilian swallowed hard. 'May I have a copy of the will, please?'

'Certainly.'

He looked at Theo who, assuming he also had to answer, said, 'Thank you very much.'

Lilian said suddenly, 'Actually, I do have a few questions.'

Nancy stood up. 'Then I'll go. Theo, will you come with me now and we'll go and say hello to people downstairs?'

He hesitated but Lilian shooed him out and the two of them descended the stairs together. In the drawing room the wake was in progress – a subdued affair with very few of the mourners present.

John Brayde came up to Nancy with Lucy and Theo willingly surrendered himself to her care. John watched them for a moment then turned to Nancy. 'No nasty shocks, I hope.'

'The will, you mean? No. As usual Papa had thought of everything. What I don't know is whether or not he was intending to – to do away with himself or was simply reacting to Lilian's desertion. I don't suppose we will ever know.' Nancy helped herself to a small sherry and sipped it absent-mindedly. She blinked back tears. 'I wish I could stop thinking about it but I can't.'

'It will take time,' he told her. 'Now, shouldn't you eat something? Food fortifies, you know.' He smiled as he led her towards the table where the food was laid out.

Cook had prepared a large game pie which had always been one of James's favourites. There was also a salad with sliced radishes, a poached salmon and a platter of eggs with mayonnaise.

Nancy shook her head. 'It's as though she expected him to share in the feast,' she murmured.

Dora fluttered past, her face flushed with excitement, a tray of glasses in her hands. Nancy was wondering what Lilian would do. She longed to confide the contents of the will to John but felt reluctantly that it would be indiscreet as well unethical. She would, however, be able to talk it over with Nanny when the last of the visitors had left.

They made their way over to the corner where Nanny had been settled. She was happily chatting with Lucy and Theo and looked up at Nancy's approach.

'It was very well done,' she declared. 'As well as could be expected in the circumstances.'

Lucy said, 'Is Theo's mama home again now? For good, I mean.'

Theo stared at her. 'Of course she is.'

'Will she let you come and share my lessons?'

Theo looked puzzled. 'Nancy said I could.'

'But your mama may not agree.'

Nancy said, 'I'm sure she will. We'll talk about it and let you know.' She winked at Nanny and held out her hand to Theo. 'If Nanny will excuse us, I have a surprise for Theo.'

Wonderingly he allowed himself to be led out of the house towards the stables, accompanied by Lucy and John. They stopped at Bay Lover's stall.

Nancy said, 'Here we are, Theo.'

He stared blankly around. 'You said there was a surprise.'

'There is.'

Willem, Bay Lover's stable lad, joined them. 'Come to see the new arrival, have you, Master Theo?' He was grinning all over his face.

'New arrival?' Lucy echoed.

He nodded. 'Can't you see how quiet Bay Lover is? Here – let me show you.'

Opening the door of the stall, John led out Bay Lover who moved forward in a slither of hooves. But there was no irritable toss of his head and no tug at his halter. The reason for this was quickly apparent as a small brown and white kid skipped out in his wake and hurried round to the horse's head.

'The little goat!' cried Theo, his face lighting up with delight.

Nancy knelt to pat the tiny creature. With its long legs, stumpy tail and small inquisitive head, it was charming.

'It's a present from Papa,' Nancy told him. 'A companion for Bay Lover, of course, but the goat is yours, Theo.'

Willem was beaming. He had kept the secret for a couple of days and was pleased at Theo's reaction. 'And see how he and Bay Lover like each other,' he enthused. 'Bay Lover isn't lonely any more.' As though to prove his point, the horse craned his neck to muzzle the small goat. 'The goat will live in the stable with Bay Lover but you can come and play with him any time you like.'

Lucy, crouching beside Theo, said, 'We'll have to think of a very special name for him.'

'His name's Button,' Theo told her. 'Mind he doesn't butt you!'

They were still grouped around the new arrival when Dora appeared at an inelegant run, the white ribbons on her cap flying.

'It's Mr Wilton, miss. He's about to leave and would like to speak to you before he goes.'

187

Nancy frowned. It was on the tip of her tongue to refuse when she decided that would be discourteous. She glanced at John Brayde. 'If you'll excuse me,' she said. 'I doubt I shall be long.'

Slowly she followed Dora back across the grass, trying to think. The events of the past few days had taken their toll and she was finding it increasingly difficult to concentrate. Lawrence's parents had stayed away from the funeral and he was probably going to pass on their regrets and excuses. She would tell him that she quite understood and would thank him for coming alone. She would be polite but distant.

He was waiting on the steps outside the French windows and hurried forward when he saw her. Dora darted away and they stood awkwardly together. This was the place, thought Nancy, where he had given her the engagement ring she had so recently returned. And this was the terrace where they had sat to plan their future. On these same steps she had grazed her knees when she fell, running away from an exasperated Nanny when she was a child. And where her father had introduced her to Lilian all those years ago.

'Thank you for coming, Lawrence.' She held out her hand. 'It was—'

He took her hand and held it. There was an urgency about him which she hadn't expected.

'Nancy, I feel we should talk, you and I. This is hardly the time or place, I know, but perhaps we could meet.'

She had never seen him so flustered and could think of nothing to say.

He went on, 'We had so much to look forward to and now . . . What I'm trying to say is . . .'

She tried to withdraw her hand but he tightened his grip. 'Please don't, Lawrence,' she said. 'It really is over between us.'

'But only if we allow it to end!' He took a step towards

188

her. 'I think we should reconsider. You mean so much to me.'

She pulled her hand free and stepped back. Keeping her voice low, she reminded him, 'When I most needed you, Lawrence, you weren't there.'

'I know, and I hate myself for it. My parents felt it was the right thing to do.' Seeing her expression, he said, 'I know now that was feeble of me. I should have stood up to them, but I didn't. You're right to blame me. But I can see everything much more clearly now.'

She held up a hand. 'Please don't go on. I've thought about this so much. I know I'm right.'

'But I must have my say, Nancy. Please let me finish. I have to explain. I don't think you meant what you said in that letter—'

'I *did*, Lawrence. I sent back your ring. Doesn't that show that I was in earnest?'

'We made a mistake. I admit it. We all should have supported you.'

'Your parents stayed away today!' she reminded him with a trace of bitterness. 'They are never going to see me as a suitable wife for you, nor as a suitable mother for your children. In their eyes I will never be more than second best. How do you think that makes me feel? How could I become part of your family knowing that I wasn't welcome?'

He stared at her desperately. 'You would do it if you loved me. Please think about it. We could go away. Start again.' He took her hand. 'Won't you give me a second chance to show how much I love you?'

Nancy discovered that she was sorry for him. She sighed heavily. 'It wouldn't be fair, Lawrence, to raise your hopes. The truth is I don't think we can ever love each other again the way we did before. And anything less wouldn't be enough, would it? We can remain good friends, can't we?' When he didn't answer she added, 'Truly, I'm sorry.'

189

The silence lengthened and his expression changed.

He said, 'It's Brayde, isn't it? I've seen—'

'No!' she said, a little too quickly. 'There's no one else. I just know that the trust is gone.'

'I've seen him looking at you, Nancy. If you haven't noticed it you must be blind!'

Nancy felt a little of her sympathy drain away and weariness made her impatient. 'John Brayde has been wonderfully supportive and I appreciate him for that. He was there when I needed a friend. Someone to lean on. Someone to offer advice and a shoulder to cry on. But I am not in love with him, nor he with me. I have no time for love, Lawrence. My days are too full of problems and my heart is full of anguish.'

She was going to say more but at that moment Lucy and Theo appeared with the young goat skipping between them. Behind them John Brayde followed at a more leisurely pace.

'I'm sorry, Lawrence,' Nancy repeated firmly and, seizing the opportunity, she reached up to kiss his cheek, then turned quickly away and started across the lawn to meet the children.

Eleven

Early that evening, when the mourners had all gone, Theo stayed at home, refusing to be parted from his mother. It seemed obvious that Lilian intended to remain at Franklins, although Nancy hesitated to ask her directly. Instead she helped Cook and Dora to clear away the remains of the food and tidy up. She assumed that Lilian would share her plans, but maybe she hadn't made up her mind.

To put some distance between them, Nancy decided to spend some time with Nanny and mentioned this to Lilian who was going through her husband's writing desk in the study.

'I hope she hasn't been overtired,' Lilian said. 'I was surprised to see her in the church.'

Still finding fault, thought Nancy.

Lilian riffled through a notebook and tossed it aside. 'Funerals can be very upsetting for elderly people.'

'She wanted to be there. She was very fond of Papa.'

Lilian shrugged and returned her attention to the contents of the desk. Just as Nancy was leaving, she asked sharply, 'Have you been going through your father's papers?'

Nancy turned back. She resented the woman's tone, which seemed to suggest that she had no right to do so. 'Of course I have. I needed to see if there were any bills to settle and there were. The butcher's account was overdue and so was the fishmonger's. I paid them both. Papa had all his work cut out with the stables. Someone had to keep the housekeeping up to date.'

'Thank you, Nancy!' Her face was flushed. 'No need to labour the point. I should have been here. It was my job. That's what you're trying to say, isn't it?'

Nancy's anger flared but she fought back a furious rejoinder. If Lilian intended to pick a quarrel with her, she would be disappointed.

'You weren't here and I took over from you. That's how it was.'

They glared at each other for a long minute, then Lilian said, 'And I suppose you rummaged through *my* desk also.'

So that was it. Now Nancy understood.

She said, 'If you're looking for the letters from Donald Cooper, they're in my room. Left-hand corner of the top drawer of the tallboy. I didn't want Papa to come across them. I knew they would hurt him.' Nancy relished the small triumph. 'I was tempted to burn them but thought you might want them.'

'You read them!' Lilian swallowed.

'Certainly not and I resent the suggestion.'

'But you *were* looking through my desk!'

'I was clearing it out. After what you'd done I was upset and angry. I wanted to be rid of you.'

There was another silence. As different emotions flitted across Lilian's face Nancy felt almost sorry for her but she told herself they had just buried her father in a shameful grave and this woman was initially to blame.

Lilian sat down suddenly on a nearby chair. 'You're hoping I'll go back to Dorset. All of you. Cook. Nanny . . . I saw it in their faces.' Her voice shook. 'I'll never be forgiven, will I?' It wasn't a question, more a statement of fact.

Nancy said quietly, 'Do you expect us to forget what you did? If you hadn't deserted Papa he'd still be alive.'

'A stronger man wouldn't have crumbled!'

'He wasn't a strong man.'

'Do you think I don't know that?' Lilian pressed a hand to her mouth.

Nancy watched her. '*Are* you going back to Cooper?'

Lilian glanced up at her. 'I don't know. I have to think of Theo. He's lost his father . . . But Donald needs me and I love him.'

'You can never bring Donald here!'

'He wouldn't come.' She sighed deeply.

What would Lilian do? Nancy wondered. Impulsively she went to her room and collected the small bundle of love letters. Returning, she tossed them into her stepmother's lap.

For a moment Lilian stared at them, then, with tears in her eyes, she picked them up and pressed them to her heart.

In spite of herself, Nancy felt a tightness in her own throat. Love was the very devil, she thought.

Lilian said, 'I don't expect you to understand.'

'Is he worth it? All the heartache!'

Instead of answering the question, Lilian said, 'I'm sorry about you and Lawrence. He wrote to Donald, you know. A very unhappy letter. I don't think their friendship is going to survive.'

Before Nancy could comment there was a rush of footsteps along the passage and a knock at the door. Both Nancy and Lilian called out, 'Come in.'

Dora appeared, her eyes bright. Ignoring Lilian, she cried, 'Oh, Miss Franklin! Jack Liddy is back and Cocksparrow won his race! The colonel won lots of money and they're back in the stableyard and it's all so . . . so wonderful!'

Nancy gasped. 'He *won*? Oh, that's marvellous news! Just what we needed. Run back down and tell him I'm on my way!' She looked at Lilian. 'Are you coming?'

The older woman shook her head. 'I don't think so. I don't think I'd be welcome, do you?'

In the stableyard the mood was one of exhilaration. Theo

193

and Lucy were there as were most of the stable lads and they set up a ragged cheer as Jack Liddy unfastened the rear of the horsebox and unloaded Cocksparrow. The four-year-old came clattering down the ramp then stood tossing his head proudly. To Nancy it seemed that the horse knew he had achieved something special. Yet she had seen him as a clumsy yearling, new from the sale ring, all spindly legs and a head that seemed too big for his body. She had stood at the paddock rail with her father, watching the young horse's antics, and had wondered at her father's choice. James, too, had had his doubts but Colonel Harding had had very little to spend that year.

'His parents are good,' her father had told her, trying to convince himself that the purchase had not been a mistake. 'Lady May out of Sarrasay. And there's something about the way he carries that great head of his. It's a gamble, Nancy, but at least the colonel didn't risk too much.'

Cocksparrow had done nothing as a two-year-old and very little in his third year. Now it seemed her father's gamble was beginning to pay off. The horse had developed late among the four-year-olds.

'Look at him! Every inch a winner!' cried Colonel Harding, his ruddy face creased in smiles. When he saw Nancy he grabbed her hand and pumped it up and down, unable to contain his enthusiasm. 'He did it, Miss Franklin! The old fellow did it!'

'Congratulations, Colonel!' she cired. 'I'm delighted for you.'

'It was such a race!' he told her. 'Your father would have loved it. He didn't look like winning. We almost didn't run him. He had that trouble with the heat in his shoulder, but Liddy thought a run might do him good. Put a bit of spirit back into him. Your father always used to say that.' He smiled. 'By the first bend Deakes was having a struggle with him. Couldn't shift the beggar! Cocksparrow didn't seem a

bit interested. He hung back and hung back and then made
a break but was closed in by Latin Lord. We thought that
was it, thought he'd lost his chance, so to speak, but then
he suddenly started to move, changed gear, Deakes says,
and he pulled forward bit by bit and suddenly he began to
move as though he was going to make a race of it.'

Jack Liddy led the horse over to be patted and fussed over
and Nancy put a hand to the soft muzzle.

'How about Gordie Brae?' she asked the colonel. Gordie
Brae belonged to John Brayde.

'Did his best but came in sixth – but there was a lot of
competition.' He patted Cocksparrow's neck, still beaming
all over his face. 'My wife was so thrilled when we led him
into the enclosure, and so were our friends. They're rather
elderly so they've headed for home to rest after all the
excitement.' He paused for breath and then he remembered
and his expression changed. 'Your father's funeral, Nancy.
How did it go? Sorry we couldn't be there but you know
how it is.'

'I understand, colonel. Papa would have wanted us all
to be there! But it's over. That's the main thing. I was
rather dreading it, as you can imagine. It was horribly
quiet and that corner of the churchyard is so . . .' The
sentence trailed away.

The colonel took hold of her hands and lowered his
voice. 'Think of it this way, Nancy. I knew your father
long before you did and I knew him man to man, as you
might say. He wouldn't give a fig for where he's buried.
He'd say one bit of grass is as good as another!' He gave
her hands a little squeeze. 'And he wouldn't want you to
grieve over it. All he'd want now is for you to put it all
behind you and get on with your life. You and that brother
of yours.'

Nancy nodded, too choked to speak. After a moment she
said, 'Well, let's celebrate. Champagne after a win. That's

what Papa would have wanted. See to the horses and we'll meet in Papa's study.'

As soon as she had uttered the words she thought about Lilian. How would she react to Nancy giving the orders? She was here at Franklins – but was she staying? Who was mistress in the house? It was difficult to know how to handle the situation.

Theo called, 'Lucy and I are going up to tell Nanny about the win. Will we have some champagne when we come down?'

'A half-glass,' Nancy promised and smiled as the two children raced together across the lawn.

Moira Callender was sitting up in bed surrounded by pillows. On the bedside table there was a small tray with the remains of a pot of tea. She was delighted to see the children and listened happily to their story of Cocksparrow's win.

She asked, 'Isn't it lovely, Theo, to have your mama home again?'

Theo nodded. 'The boys at school said she'd run away but she hadn't. I knew she hadn't. But I don't have to go back to that school. I can have lessons with Lucy. Nancy said so.'

Lucy caught Moira's eye and they exchanged a worried glance. Would Lilian agree to the plan? To change the subject, Moira said, 'Who wants to play Snakes and Ladders? I feel like a game before I settle down to sleep.'

They had just laid out the board when there was a knock at the door and Lilian came in. Theo jumped up and ran to hug her and Nanny watched with a tightness in her throat.

'I have to talk to Nanny,' Lilian told them. 'Theo and Lucy, you must play the game some other time.'

Theo pouted but Lucy said, 'Never mind, Theo. We'll go downstairs and join in the celebrations!' She winked at him and, remembering the champagne, he gave in gracefully.

196

When they were alone, Lilian said, 'May I sit with you? We need to talk.'

Startled, Moira nodded, unable to hide her apprehension. A talk with Lilian? Such a thing was unheard of.

Lilian pulled up a chair and sat by the bed. 'You were at the reading of the will,' she said without preamble. 'I'm not here about your future. You will stay here. It's about Nancy. You see, *I* have a choice to make – a choice which affects us all. I have to decide whether to stay here and bring up Theo or to follow my heart and marry Donald Cooper.'

'A difficult decision.' Moira's expression was not encouraging. She had pulled the bedcovers up around her defensively.

Lilian ignored the jibe. 'You know the girl better than anyone. Certainly better than I do. I need to know how she's feeling. I can't talk to her. She's so prickly. She hates me and although I understand—'

'Nancy's a sweet girl. She doesn't hate anybody!'

'Except me. She's never accepted me and I can live with that. I have done for a long time. She resents me and thinks I've replaced her in James's affections.'

'You seem to know all about her. Why do you need my opinion?'

Lilian stood up and crossed to the window. 'I want to stay with Theo. I want to keep Franklins going for Theo's sake but I can't do it alone.' She turned and her expression was bleak. 'I certainly can't do it if everybody is against me, as I suspect they are.'

'By "everybody" you mean Nancy, I suppose.'

'By everybody I mean *everybody*!' She drew in a breath and let it out slowly. 'I mean you and Nancy and Cook and Jack Liddy and the Symeses and . . . They all blame me for James's death.'

'And you want to know if they will ever forgive and

forget?' The old lady shook her head. 'I can't tell you that because I have no idea. I'm sorry.'

'But you can tell me if *you* are willing to help me.' Lilian recrossed the room and sat down. 'If you spoke to Nancy . . . She respects you. If she would work with me instead of against me I think the others might be won over. I don't ever expect anyone to love me. That would be too much to hope for.'

Behind the bravado Moira sensed a note of regret and looked at her curiously.

Lilian continued, 'If I stay I sacrifice a great deal.' She closed her eyes at the thought of what she would lose. Before Moira could speak she opened them again. 'If I am to stay I need some help.'

'You should talk to Nancy yourself. It's not fair to ask me.'

'I'm not interested in what is and isn't fair!' cried Lilian, her voice rising. 'I'm interested in my son's future and mine and Franklins'. I'm not used to all this responsibility. If I take it on it will be a huge burden. Nancy will marry at some time and I'll be on my own. I don't know if I can do it.'

She put her hands over her face and Moira was surprised by a frisson of compassion. Disaster had certainly humbled Lilian Franklin. But this *was* the Lilian who had tried to persuade James to get rid of a useless old nanny. Could she possibly preserve Franklins for Theo? Did they want her to try?

She said, 'I can't help you, Lilian, because I can't speak for the others. All I can say is that Nancy will do anything for Theo. If she sees that you have Theo's best interests at heart, you may well win her over.'

'You really think so?' Lilian's tone was doubtful. 'We shall see.' She stood up.

Moira said, 'I wasn't much help. I'm—'

'No, you weren't.' Lilian shrugged. 'But thank you for trying.'

She swept from the room leaving Nanny to stare after her, bewildered and not a little confused.

When Nancy entered the breakfast room next morning she was surprised to find Lilian already there. Theo was not present but Nancy guessed he had eaten early and rushed down to the stables to play with his new pet.

Lilian was spreading honey on a slice of brown bread and she was, as always, immaculate. A cream blouse flattered her pale complexion and Nancy thought she detected a trace of rouge on her cheeks. Her father would have disapproved, thought Nancy. Make-up was for painted women. He had been rather old-fashioned in that respect.

Resisting the inclination to ignore her stepmother, Nancy asked, 'Did you sleep well?'

'With *my* conscience, you mean?'

Nancy meant exactly that but she said, 'No. It was just a polite question.'

Lilian's expression darkened. She had recognised the lie. Don't underestimate her, Nancy told herself.

'There's a lot you don't know about me, Nancy,' Lilian told her. 'And a lot you don't know about your father. We have to talk, you and I. We have to get it out into the open if we are ever to have—'

'I don't want to talk to you about Papa!' Nancy said sharply. She sat down with a slice of bacon and three grilled tomatoes. 'I'd like to eat my breakfast in peace.'

'I'd like to spend the rest of my life in peace but it isn't very likely!'

Nancy told herself not to be drawn into an argument. In a lighter tone she said, 'I'm sorry you couldn't join us for the champagne last night. Cocksparrow surprised everyone. It was good to have something to be cheerful about.'

Lilian gave Nancy a shrewd look. 'I suppose you believe your father was perfect. Many daughters do.'

'I told you – I don't want to—'

'I expect you think I chased him for his money. Oh, don't bother to pretend. I know what people said about me.'

Dora came in and Nancy said, 'Take my plate, Dora, will you. I've lost my appetite.'

With a nervous glance in Lilian's direction, Dora did so. 'Cook says do you want anything else? More hot water?'

Lilian and Nancy spoke together to say, 'No thank you.'

Nancy bit back her irritation. Having left Franklins, Lilian had the gall to return as though nothing had happened. The woman was beyond belief.

Lilian went on, 'I was in love with Donald Cooper when I first met your father.'

Suddenly Nancy was intrigued although she tried not to show it.

'I thought he was in love with me – Donald, I mean. I adored him. I thought we would marry, but suddenly he began to take an interest in another young woman and I was very hurt. You may not believe it but I do have feelings.'

Nancy stared out of the window, feigning indifference.

'Your father fell in love with me – or became infatuated with me. I'm not sure with hindsight which way it was. As the weeks went on I would say he became obsessed. I was flattered and I needed the attention. My self-confidence was at a rather low ebb. Gradually we spent more and more time together but all the time I was hoping Donald would come back to me.'

Nancy thought about Lawrence and his rejection. Yes, she thought reluctantly, I do know how it feels.

Lilian sighed. 'In the end I couldn't bring myself to hurt your father. When he proposed I said yes. I thought I could make him happy.'

'*Did* you make him happy?'

200

'I imagine so. But I soon realised that I came a poor
second to Franklins. We hardly saw each other during the
day. He wanted me to ride but I wasn't keen on the idea. I
preferred to read and entertain and dance. More the social
butterfly. We had nothing in common.'

'And then you had Theo.' It sounded like an accusation.

'I had Theo. Not from choice, I'm afraid, but from
carelessness. I was afraid of childbirth and I didn't want
any children. I told James that and he agreed reluctantly.
Then – lo and behold! I presented him with a son and heir.
Nanny did her bit again but I felt trapped.'

Now Nancy was watching her stepmother closely. It all
sounded feasible but was it true? Or was Lilian putting a
different slant on everything? She couldn't tell.

Lilian put her elbows on the table and steepled her hands.
She *was* very beautiful, Nancy admitted. She could see how
her father might have become infatuated with her. But how
could Donald have become disenchanted? Unless Lilian had
wanted marriage and he had resisted, preferring to keep his
freedom.

'Years later Donald suddenly started showing an interest
again. I was in an impossible situation. A dilemma, to put
it mildly. James was becoming bored with me and I had
never stopped loving Donald. We drifted into an affair very
easily because we already meant a lot to each other. The rest
you know.'

After a long silence Nancy asked, 'And now you want
Theo?'

'Yes, I do. I thought I could live without him . . . but
anyway, James wouldn't part with him. Now Donald refuses
to bring up another man's child.' She looked at Nancy and
her eyes were anguished. 'And Franklins is Theo's heritage.
I want to stay here with him. But it all depends on you. If
you are going to fight me all the way I'll fail and the stables
will fail. I want to ask Liddy to take over as trainer. We

201

may or may not succeed but one thing I do know—' She
gave Nancy a hard stare. 'We have to get to grips with
the problem immediately. Already owners are considering
removing their horses. We have to decide now.' When
Nancy still didn't reply she said, 'I'm not expecting you
to devote your life to the stables, Nancy. You'll marry
someone. Maybe not Lawrence Wilton. Who knows. But
I need you *with me*, in both meanings of the words, for at
least a year.'

Nancy was aware of the beginnings of admiration. Lilian
was showing unexpected courage. Also the revelations about
her earlier romance with Cooper did cast a slightly kinder
light on her recent actions. Nancy appreciated the confi-
dences – but could she bear to spend another year in this
woman's company?

Stalling for time, she said, 'Nothing changes the fact that
if it weren't for you Papa would still be alive. You can't
expect me to forgive that. Or to forget.'

'You're obviously determined not to do so!' Lilian's
expression was part bitterness, part resignation. 'I shall never
forgive myself, but that's of no interest to anyone else.'

She stood up, tossing her napkin on to the table. 'Perhaps
you'd think things over and let me know your decision.'

'And if I say no?'

'I'll face that problem when and if it comes.' At the
door Lilian hesitated. 'Are you sleeping, Nancy? You look
very tired.'

Surprised, Nancy said, 'Not well but enough.'

'You had a terrible shock, finding James the way you did
and then dealing with the aftermath. It can weaken you, you
know, physically. My mother found her sister dead in bed.
She had taken arsenic. Mother never really recovered. It
affected her nerves.'

'Arsenic? How dreadful!' Nancy was distracted by the
information. 'But why did she do it?'

202

'She suffered all her life from a severe melancholy. She had tried once before to kill herself.' Lilian shrugged. 'I remember my mother screaming hysterically.'

'So was she buried in a . . . another part of the church-yard?'

'Sadly, yes. They were even stricter in those days.' She sighed. 'I've asked the doctor to call and see you after his rounds. Just to reassure myself that you're not overtaxing your strength. I hope you don't mind. This is a difficult time for all of us and it pays to be careful.'

She closed the door behind her, leaving Nancy staring after her, more perplexed than ever.

Dr Loman had been the Franklins' doctor ever since Nancy could remember. Now he was in his fifties, stout and with a beard and failing eyesight, but Nancy could recall him as a younger man with dark curls and darker eyes.

He found her in the garden, on her hands and knees, uprooting a rhododendron shoot.

'My dear young Miss Franklin! How very unladylike!' He deposited his bag on the grass and held out a hand to help her up. He had always teased her and she and Theo had liked him enormously.

Nancy stood, one hand to her head.

'Dizzy?' he asked and she nodded.

'Don't overdo it,' he reminded her.

She held out the plant, which had sprouted a few roots. 'Do you think this will take?' she asked. 'I want to plant it near Papa's grave. He loved the salmon pink best of all – not that he had much time for gardening, but Mama used to drag him round, insisting that he admire her handiwork.'

'Your mother was very creative. She liked everything to be as attractive as possible. Even the garden was a challenge to her.' He took the plant from Nancy and examined it through his round spectacles. 'I imagine it'll be all right

203

– if you keep it watered until it gets a hold in the soil.'
He returned it to her. 'I'm sorry I couldn't be with you
at the funeral. Mrs Finch went into labour early and the
midwife wasn't happy to be on her own. Mrs Finch nearly
lost her first child and we expected complications – and
got them!'

'Complications? Is the baby all right?'

'It was touch and go, but I think so. And the funeral?'

She gestured dismissively with her hands. 'Very subdued.
Understated might be the right word.' She laid the plant in a
small trug. 'I'm not asking permission to plant these,' she
confessed. 'It might be refused. I prefer to slide them in
unannounced.'

He glanced round. 'Young Theo – how's he bearing up,
poor lad?'

'I think he's fine. Lucy Brayde is mothering him a
little and we've given him a kid to keep his attention.
Something to love.' She smiled faintly. 'You remember
his old wooden horse? He gave it to Papa. Laid it in his
coffin.' She swallowed as the memory of her father's face
came back to her. 'Papa looked very peaceful. After that
morning . . . Well! That's all in the past, isn't it.'

'And you? Your stepmother is concerned about you. She
thinks you are overtaxing your strength.'

Nancy's jaw tensed. 'It's a bit late in the day for her
to start caring. She should have cared more about Papa!'
She avoided the doctor's eyes, aware of how spiteful she
sounded.

'Is it ever too late to start caring?' he asked mildly,
watching a mistlethrush searching for grubs among the
grass. When Nancy didn't answer he said, 'It was good
of you to take George Symes back. They're a nice family
and work is hard to come by.'

'I understood Papa's dilemma where Lilian was concerned – and he also has an ulcer, poor man.'

'A strict diet will improve matters.' He gave Nancy a searching glance and said, 'I want to tell you something in confidence, Nancy. Could you bear it, do you think? I wouldn't want you to repeat it.'

She was at once alarmed but said, 'I can. Is it about Lilian?'

'Only indirectly. It's about your father. I know you blame Lilian for the fact that he took his own life. You may need to reconsider when I tell you—' He frowned then sighed. 'Your father made me swear to keep it a secret but in the circumstances . . . He came to me about a year ago with stomach pains and after some tests I told him it was a tumour.'

'Oh no!' Nancy stared at him. 'Not Papa.'

'I'm afraid so. He knew his life expectancy was not very good but he wouldn't tell anyone. Not even his wife.'

'Lilian didn't know? Oh, poor Papa! It must have been so lonely.'

'He thought Lilian would be frightened. I had to agree with him there. Your stepmother has a fear of all things medical, although she does her best to hide it. When Theo was on the way she made herself ill with worry, convinced she would die giving birth. Do you remember when Theo had chicken pox? It was a nightmare for her.'

'I know she left it to Nanny to care for him.'

'Now you know why.' He thrust his hands into his pockets. 'I'm telling you this because I can see that your father's prognosis might have contributed to his desire to die. It was certainly the reason why he told no one about the cancer.' He sighed. 'It may be that Lilian's disappearance with that bounder Cooper decided him, but it would only have been a contributory factor. Not the main reason that your father . . . did what he did. That and the drinking, of course. He swore that a large whisky was the only thing that truly dulled the pain. I'm not saying that he wouldn't have killed himself if he'd been sober, but put it this way, Nancy. The cancer began the downward spiral.' He picked up his bag and squared his shoulder. 'Come by the surgery tomorrow and collect a sleeping draught – for you and for Lilian. You both need a good night's sleep. And now let me take a quick look at young Theo before I get on home.'

'He's down at the stables,' Nancy told him.

'Now why am I not surprised?' he answered, smiling, and they walked down together.

Twelve

Nancy spent a restless night struggling with her conscience. Lilian's candour had taken her by surprise and her words had undermined Nancy's negative feelings towards her. Part of her now wanted to help Lilian with the management of Franklins, but somehow that felt like a defeat. That would make Lilian a winner and that rankled. Nancy had resented Lilian ever since their first meeting, when her girlish intuition had warned her that the woman was vying with her for James's affection. Nancy had sulked throughout the wedding and had ignored Nanny's whispered insistence that she 'pull herself together' and 'put a brave face on things'. She had not done either and had maintained an air of aloof indifference towards her stepmother. That way, she felt, she could remain loyal to her own dead mother and make life difficult for Lilian, who had usurped her. Even at the time she had known in her heart that her behaviour was shabby and now she was dismayed to feel a deep sense of shame. Was it any wonder, she thought, that Lilian had never taken to her stepdaughter? Nancy had never given her a chance.

Nancy also saw quite clearly that her father would wish his daughter to mend bridges and that if she failed to do so Lilian would not succeed at Franklins. Which meant that Franklins would no longer be a leading racing stables and there would be nothing for Theo when he came of age.

Still sleepless, she turned over, trying to make herself

comfortable in the bed. Tired of the problem, she tried to think about Lawrence and his request that they try again with the relationship. She knew she ought to be willing but the thought gave her no pleasure and it seemed unlikely that they would ever recover the original magic. They had been passionately in love and it had cooled. It had fallen apart at the first hurdle and that hardly boded well for the future. She had tried to convince him on the day of the funeral but maybe she should put pen to paper again.

'I'll write to him,' she murmured. 'A nice letter promising to remain good friends.'

For a few moments she attempted to write the letter in her head, putting together suitable phrases which effectively said no without hurting Lawrence's feelings or damaging his confidence. He was basically a kind man and his heart was in the right place. She was tempted to get up and write the letter then and there but a glance at the bedside clock showed her it was past midnight and she decided it would have to wait until morning.

Turning over yet again Nancy allowed herself to think about John Brayde, allowing her memories of him to re-surface. When they did she relived each one and examined her feelings towards him. There was no point in denying that she found him attractive or that he seemed to enjoy her company.

'I think he does like me,' she whispered. Perhaps she should encourage him in some way. She could suggest to Lilian that he and Lucy come to dinner one evening. But then he didn't care for Lilian and she might resent him because he and Cooper had never been friendly. Nancy sighed. It was so difficult to know what to do.

She stretched and snuggled deeper beneath the sheets and her eyelids fluttered sleepily but almost at once she was awake again and thinking about Lilian. She would have to swallow her pride, she decided reluctantly. It made no sense for her to be small-minded at such a time. First thing in the morning she would tell Lilian. She would promise to stay for a year. After that she would reconsider her options. Having finally reached a conclusion she smiled tiredly into the darkness and slipped into a dreamless sleep.

Awake at five past six, she sat up and rubbed her eyes. Remembering her decision, she was at once enthused by the idea and determined to tell Lilian immediately. In slippered feet, she pulled on her dressing gown and padded silently along the passage to her father's room. A knock on the door brought no response so she knocked again and then cautiously opened the door. The large bed was empty. So, Lilian had also risen early. Nancy hurried along to the bathroom but drew another blank. Puzzled, she went downstairs to the kitchen where Cook, the bellows in her hand, was encouraging the coals in the range. Dora was tucking her hair up beneath her cap with the aid of a small mirror.

'Good morning,' said Nancy. 'I'm looking for Mrs Franklin. She's not in her room and I—'

Cook said, 'You've missed her. She's gone down to the stables. Been gone nearly an hour.'

'The stables? At this time?' Nancy stared at her.

Dora said, 'She's going to ride out with Mr Liddy to watch the first string at the gallops.'

'At the . . . !' Nancy was astonished. 'But Lilian doesn't ride! She's never even wanted to learn.'

'She's learning now,' said Cook, heaving herself to her feet. 'And you, Dora, get that hot-water jug up to the bedroom for Miss Nancy. She'll be wanting to wash.'

Minutes later, when the hot water had been delivered, Cook and Dora settled down to a cup of tea.

'Three sugars,' said Cook.

'Yesterday it was two!'

'Different spoon and don't answer back.'

209

Dora waited for the right moment to share her news with
Cook. At last she said, 'Mr Symes's nephew is staying with
them. Alfred, his name is. He's giving Mr Symes a hand
while he's poorly.'

Cook gave her a suspicious look. 'Well, don't go getting
any ideas about him. How old is he?'

'Seventeen.' Dora blew on her tea.

'A boy can be a man at seventeen so watch your step,
Dora.'

'He says Mr Symes is waiting for the mistress to start
gallivanting again. He doesn't know—'

Cook leaned forward, wagging her finger. 'You mind your
tongue, Dora, and act respectful.'

'But I only said what you said—'

'That was *before*, you silly girl. When she'd left Franklins.
Now she's back again.'

'You mean she might stay?'

'Of course she might. And it wasn't her took you on,
remember. It was Miss Franklin. So keep your thoughts to
yourself unless you want to get your cards sooner rather
than later.'

Dora looked crushed. 'I only said—'

'And don't get tangled up with any nephews. If there's
one thing mistresses hate it's followers!'

'I know something else,' Dora told her. 'About Miss
Franklin and Mr Brayde. Theo says that Lucy says that Mr
Brayde says—'

'Spit it out, girl!'

'That one day he might ask Miss Franklin to marry him.
Theo says Lucy says—'

Cook groaned but Dora ignored her.

'Lucy says he's lonely and Lucy wants him to marry her
so that she can be Theo's sister. When Lucy asked him he
didn't say he would but he didn't say he wouldn't.'

Cook was beaming. 'Theo told you all that? Well, he's

a monkey and no mistake. You'd best keep it to yourself.'

'I haven't told a soul!'

'You've just told me . . . but wouldn't it be a turn-up for the books? They'd make a lovely couple even though he is older than her.'

'Better than Mr Lawrence? He's ever so handsome.'

Cook struggled to her feet. 'Handsome is as handsome does!' she said mysteriously. 'But now we've got things to do. We'd best make a start.'

Nancy went back upstairs, pondering the miracle. Lilian was already up and about, riding out to oversee the gallops! She was torn between irritation and admiration. Too late, she wished that *she* had risen early and gone down to the stables. At least she could ride, although she hadn't chosen to do so for many years.

'Good for you!' she told the absent Lilian and made up her mind to join her.

When the water arrived she gave herself a brief wash and dressed quickly. Ten minutes later she arrived in the stableyard, to the consternation of the remaining lads who were preparing to ride out with the second string as soon as the others returned. The stableyard was never at its best at this hour in the morning. Dirty straw had been raked out from the stalls and stood in steaming heaps just beyond the yard. Buckets were piled near the pump. Blankets were being aired and most of the stall doors stood open. Bridles and saddles were being carried out from the tack room and one or two horses were already saddled and were pawing at the cobbles, impatient to be off. Horses stood at various angles across the yard while sweating lads applied brushes and combs in preparation for their outing. If the animals weren't 'as near perfect as dammit', Jack Liddy would have something to say about it.

'Morning, Miss Nancy!' Fred looked up, red-faced. He was working on Musket with the brush. The horse turned his head enquiringly and Nancy patted his sleek head.

'We're up with the lark this morning,' she said and laughed rather self-consciously. 'I thought you lads would like some company too, so I'll be riding out with you – if you've got a suitable hack.'

They exchanged delighted grins and Nancy suddenly realised that they had felt the first string to be honoured by Lilian's interest. For a moment she wondered how the lads had reacted to Lilian's return but then banished the thought. If she and Lilian were to cooperate she must put the memory of those days behind her.

Fred said, 'You can take Mrs Franklin's mount when she gets back. Tad'll love another outing.'

'Thank you. I'll do that.'

Fred shouted, 'They're coming back now. Look lively!' and there was a last-minute rush to give the horses their final polish and tidy the yard.

The first string of horses came clattering back, their sides heaving, their eyes rolling, still excited from their morning exercise. Lilian too looked flushed with success but Jack Liddy looked his normal thoughtful self. The lads, however, were smiling broadly. One by one they slid to the ground. Saddles were removed and the horses chuntered cheerfully, aware that after their grooming they would be fed.

Nancy went forward to help Lilian dismount. 'Well done!' she whispered.

Once on the ground Lilian clung to Nancy's arm for a moment as she reoriented herself. 'My legs are shaking,' she confessed.

'But you stayed on!'

Jack Liddy said, 'The mistress did very well.'

She said, 'Tad looked after me,' and patted the animal's neck.

Fred said, 'He's going to look after Miss Nancy now.'
Lilian looked at Nancy, wide-eyed. 'You are riding out?'
Nancy nodded. 'Yes. You beat me to it. *I* was going to
surprise *you*.' They regarded each other warily.

Nancy kept her eyes on Lilian's and saw hope flicker.
'I thought about what you said and it makes good sense.
We need to be on the same side.' She smiled suddenly and
lowered her voice. 'Two women against the world! It's the
only way, isn't it.'

Suddenly Nancy longed to say how sorry she was for
all the bad feeling that had existed between them in the
past, but this was not the time nor the place. It would
wait, she decided, but it must be said some time. The
slate must be wiped clean in readiness for their fresh
start.

Lilian smiled. 'I'm so pleased, Nancy.'

She made a slight move towards Nancy and then hesitated.
But Nancy knew intuitively what the older woman had
intended and impulsively she leaned forward and gave her a
quick hug. It was a small gesture but significant. Lilian was
no longer her stepmother, but her friend – and that meant a
new beginning for all of them.

August 1904

Early one morning, Mrs Bailey arrived at Franklin Manor
in a contented frame of mind. Later, after a cup of tea and a
slice of carroway cake, she knelt in the drawing room with
the sun streaming in at the window. Fate had been kind to
her, there was no doubt about that. A year ago she had
been generously compensated for Nancy's half-completed
wedding dress when the marriage was called off. A month
later she had managed to alter the style so that she could
sell it to another bride. Now she was back at Franklins,

213

pinning up the hem of a second gown. This one would be less intricate than the other with one layer of pale coffee satin and some silver beadwork across the hem and shoulders. But it would look beautiful, she reflected, her lips clamped over the inevitable row of pins. Funny how things work out.

She gave a little tug on the material and Nancy turned obediently.

Nancy said, 'Only three weeks. It doesn't seem possible, does it.'

Mrs Bailey shook her head and pushed the last pin into place around the hem.

'And you're definitely going for the white roses?' she asked.

'I think so . . . or maybe cream.'

At that moment Theo came into the room. He stared in consternation at the sight before him. 'I'm sorry,' he said. 'I didn't know you were in here.'

Mrs Bailey sat back and looked at him fondly. He had grown in the past year in more ways than one. He had always been so shy and nervous, but he was more confident now. Yet just as good-looking! Just like his mother, she admitted reluctantly. Mrs Bailey, like many others, had been unwilling to accept Lilian Franklin's return, but a year was a long time and the woman had surprised them by her dedication to the stables.

Nancy smiled at him. 'Say hello to Mrs Bailey, Theo!'

He turned guiltily. 'Hello, Mrs Bailey.'

'Hello, Master Theo.' He'll be a heartbreaker when he's older, she thought.

Nancy said, 'Now that you're here you can tell me what you think of my dress.'

He gave the question serious consideration. 'Very nice,' he said finally. 'Has Lucy seen it?'

'No, but she can have a peep one day if she wants to. But

214

not John.' Nancy rolled her eyes theatrically. 'The wedding dress has to be a secret from the groom.'

Mrs Bailey struggled upright and stood back, admiring her handiwork. The bottom of the skirt appeared to be level and she sighed with satisfaction. She would hem it after her midday meal.

Theo said, 'Cook has made sausage rolls and ham sandwiches. She says to ask you if that's all.'

Mrs Bailey raised her eyebrows. 'Is there a party going on?'

Theo grinned, full of importance. 'It's a barn party. Lucy's and mine. Lucy's housekeeper is making some biscuits and some orange jellies and Mr Symes's children are coming – except the baby, who's too young . . . and Tim is going to play his concertina, and we're hanging paper lanterns across the barn so that when it starts to get dark they'll shine!'

'Well, you are lucky!' Mrs Bailey reached out to pat his head but he dodged smartly and Nancy laughed.

'Tell Cook that sausage rolls and ham sandwiches will be plenty and remember to say thank you.'

Theo nodded, his eyes still on the dressmaker. 'We were going to have it last summer for Lucy's birthday, but . . . but Papa died.' His face darkened momentarily. 'And then Nanny died. But this year nobody has died so we can have the party.' He turned to Nancy. 'Where's Mama?'

'In the office. But she and Mr Liddy are busy with next month's race plans. Can it wait?'

Theo nodded and hurried out of the room.

'He's a little love!' said Mrs Bailey. 'Reminds me of my Tom when he was that age. And now he's twenty-seven! How the years do fly . . . And I hear Master Theo's getting his own pony for Christmas.'

'Probably before then. We were going to advertise, but Mr Brayde has heard of one that might be suitable.' She pulled on her skirt and tucked in her blouse.

215

Mrs Bailey hesitated. She had one more snippet of news to impart but wondered about how it would be received. Busying herself with the packing of the skirt, she folded it carefully into layers of tissue paper. Casually she said, 'Have you heard about Mr Wilton? They say he's—'

'Courting the vet's daughter? Yes.' Nancy tidied her hair. 'Her father told us a few weeks back. Splendid news, isn't it? Mr Evans is delighted and I'm sure the Wiltons will approve of Harriet. If you're sure you haven't time for tea and biscuits—?'

'I'd love to say yes but I'm run off my feet this month.'

Nancy glanced round. 'Don't forget your sewing bag.'

Five minutes later Mrs Bailey had settled her parcel into the carrier of her bicycle and was wobbling away down the drive.

Nancy watched her go and glanced again at the clock. Nearly eleven. John was coming to take her into town. He was determined to buy her a locket to celebrate the recent win at Newmarket. Blue Boy had surprised everyone by romping home a clear head in front of the opposition in spite of a late start. It wasn't a large prize but it was unexpected. She and John would shop and then they would have lunch in their favourite hotel.

Upstairs Nancy freshened up and changed her blouse. She had just tidied her hair when she heard the crunch of wheels on the drive outside and she flew down the stairs and out of the front door. John was waiting at the bottom of the steps and she ran down to him, smiling broadly.

He said, 'Nancy! My love!'

'John!'

And then she was in his arms and he was swinging her off the ground. As they kissed a wonderful feeling of contentment filled her. The worst was over and she had survived. In fact, she had emerged a stronger person with a deeper understanding of the world and its ways. For the first time since her father's death she knew she was stepping from the shadows into the light. She tightened her arms around John's broad back. This was the man with whom she would share her life, and her father would have approved.

Gently John released her and, standing back a little, smiled down at her.

'It's good to see you so happy,' he said.

Nancy took his hands in hers and pressed them to her lips.

'I'm not just happy,' she told him. 'At this moment I'm in love with the whole world!'